SNOW

Also by Meera Trehan:

The View from the Very Best House in Town

WALKER
BOOKS

This is a work of fiction. Names, characters, places and incidents are either the product of the author's imagination or, if real, used fictitiously. All statements, activities, stunts, descriptions, information and material of any other kind contained herein are included for entertainment purposes only and should not be relied on for accuracy or replicated as they may result in injury.

First published 2025 by Walker Books Ltd
87 Vauxhall Walk, London SE11 5HJ

2 4 6 8 10 9 7 5 3 1

EU Authorized Representative: HackettFlynn Ltd, 36 Cloch Choirneal, Balrothery, Co. Dublin, K32 C942, Ireland. EU@walkerpublishinggroup.com

This book has been typeset in Manticore

Printed and bound by CPI Group (UK) Ltd, Croydon CR0 4YY

British Library Cataloguing in Publication Data:
a catalogue record for this book is available from the British Library

ISBN 978-1-5295-2878-7

www.walker.co.uk

FSC www.fsc.org
MIX
Paper | Supporting responsible forestry
FSC® C013604

FOR CURT,
WHO LOVES SCIENCE AND SNOW

Announcement of the Royal Birth

Let it be known in every corner of the great and noble Kingdom of Mistmir – from the tallest highland peaks to the lowest riverbanks, from the bustling city to the fertile farmlands – that today, on the first day of winter, our esteemed and beloved King and Queen have welcomed a healthy baby girl,

KARINA.

May the Mists protect our new Princess always!
May her every wish come true!

Part One

The Princess
and the
Snow

1

The Princess

A VERY ODD FOOT

You've likely heard a million things about the Princess, all bad, most true, and the fact that she's a liar is just one. But it's the King's honest truth that she is simply digging one last shovelful of Snow for the evening when out of nowhere appears a giant foot. To be precise, there is a leg attached to the foot, and it comes through the Boundary Mists, which is possibly not nowhere.

The Princess blinks. She squints. She rubs her eyes, certain that the Snow or the loneliness or the endless digging has finally led her to start seeing things. But the foot is still there. It drops in the Snow, then lifts back up, leaving a large print. For a split second, the Princess holds completely still. She wills the Snow to do the same. As always, it ignores her. With a hiss and a whine, it fills the footprint back up, erasing it. But it was there. Just because the Snow covered it up doesn't mean it wasn't. Enough Snow can conceal anything.

The Princess blinks again, and the foot reappears, sinking in just a finger's-width from where it first stepped. On second glance, she realizes the foot itself is a normal size, but it's encased in some sort of garishly coloured contraption with a metal frame that makes its print very large. It moves carefully, like whoever the foot belongs to doesn't trust the Snow. Which means they might be smarter than you'd guess from their ridiculous footwear.

The Princess stares into the thick Mists, waiting for the whole person to come through, forcing her eyes to focus and her stomach to settle. She knows it can't be one of her subjects. First, she's not naive enough to think that any of the people who fled the Snow – or, really, her – would return on a whim. And second, no self-respecting citizen of Mistmir would wear a shoe that silly in public. But the idea of having anyone visit, anyone to talk to, makes the Princess a little giddy.

To be clear, she would rather have all her subjects return, her kingdom restored to what it once was. That is what she truly wants – to be a real princess again. Of course it is. It's what she was born to do, it's what she's been trained to do, it's what she's been working for, tirelessly and endlessly. It's her duty and her prize, as the King likes to tell her. (True, he's also her father, but you'd call him the King too, even if he were your flesh and blood.) But the idea that she might not be alone while she works... She knows she's not supposed to make wishes anymore, but she may have secretly wished for that.

She waits for the visitor. No one comes. Instead, the foot disappears again, and the Princess is struck by the fact that she may never see its owner – or anyone else – ever again.

She sprints after them. The Snow behind her wails, and the Mists get closer and closer until they're swirling instead of solid, and she realizes she might actually make it through the passing point. It doesn't matter that it's supposed to be impossible; she's going to leave, she's going to see this person, and she—

—lands squarely on her bottom. The Mists repel her like she's some sort of pest.

She sits in the Snow for a moment to let her head clear. The Snow buzzes against her coat and gloves, sending her small reminders of where she is – her kingdom. Of who she is – the Princess. Of what she almost did – abandon the Kingdom of Mistmir to chase a very odd foot. Put it that way, she has to laugh. A foot! Even a princess can be silly, see?

She stands up, dusts off, and plasters her royal smile on her face, just as she's been taught to do. It's muscle memory. She bends down to pick up her shovel. It's then she realizes that the odd foot has been replaced by a hand in a fat mitten rummaging through the Snow. The person it belongs to can't be more than an arm's-length away. If it weren't for the solid fog, she could look them in the eye or squeeze their shoulder or beg them to stay. Even if she has been taught better than to beg.

"Please come in," she says.

The hand freezes in midair. The Princess holds her breath the way she sometimes does the moment after she digs a hole, before it can fill, and thinks: *This is the moment the Snow will change back to ordinary snow. This is the moment when winter ends. This is the moment when our kingdom goes back to what it once was. This is the moment when I'll be forgiven.*

But, sure as the Snow, the hand draws back as if it's been burned. The Princess doesn't have a chance to say another word, not "wait" or "stay" or even one more "please", before the holes in the Snow and the holes in the Mists close up and she's left alone against the edge of her kingdom. She stands in the moonlight, surveying the endless, relentless, perfect Snow. Not a flake out of place. Just what she wished for.

Her gift to herself, right?

2

The Princess

THE COLOUR OF SNOW

The first rays of sun shine silver through the ice-bricks of the Gardener's Cottage. It's still called that even though the gardener was one of the first to leave Mistmir. It didn't take him long to figure out that endless snow was probably not advantageous to his long-term job prospects. But the Princess can't bear to call it the Princess's Cottage, even if in reality that is what it is. Admitting that out loud would be like admitting that her kingdom is permanently lost. It's hard enough to dig every day without that thought.

The Princess untangles herself from her blankets and blinks away the last of her dreams. She stretches her arms and hits an out-of-place shovel. It falls to the floor with a clatter. She sits up with a start. And then she remembers. The odd foot, the fat mitten – *those* weren't dreams. Last night, for the first time in a long time, something happened. Someone – or, more precisely, part of someone – came to Mistmir.

And if they did it once, they might do it again.

The Princess splashes water on her face, brushes her teeth with mint-grass powder, and runs a boar-cupine-bristle brush through her hair. Though the handle is broken, it works well enough. She leaves on her gold key necklace and ties her hair back with a red ribbon. She learned early on that she couldn't stop being the Princess just because everyone had left, even if she is the reason they're gone. When other people are here, you do these things so they don't forget who you are. When you're all alone, you do them so you don't. Besides, if her subjects ever return – or, rather, when they do – she will need to look presentable every day. Best not to get too out of practise.

She gulps down a couple of hard ginger-spice biscuits and a cup of cold water. Her strap-sack is a tangled mess, but she makes quick work of the knots, and soon she's packed a shovel, a rake and some smaller trowels. It may be more than she needs, but she's not about to lose her chance to find any clues this Stranger may have left.

Strap-sack on and coat buttoned, the Princess heads into the morning. As always, Snow blankets the ground, but the sky is cloudless. The Princess studied her science lessons well enough to know why, in this Snow-filled land, it doesn't even snow anymore. She remembers the diagram her tutor, Madame Vidya, drew about the role moisture plays in generating wind, and the role wind plays in generating weather. Without water droplets evaporating or melting, the weather can't change. Every day becomes the same.

Even so, the Snow seems different today, glowing pink in the new-morning light. Soon it will turn orange, then gold, then a white so bright it will sparkle, except in the shadows. There it will be a frigid blue. The King once called the Snow monotonous, but looking out at the Snowfields, the Princess disagrees. "Mono" means one and "tone" means colour, and the words combined mean boring. This Snow is neither single coloured nor boring. Not when there's a spark of hope to light it.

3

The Princess

MUSCLE MEMORY

The Princess is not worried about what she will say when she meets this person. Not at all. Madame Vidya taught her well: not just academics, but etiquette too – essential knowledge for all royalty.

The Princess rattles off the list as she strides down the hill toward the Mists. Not that she needs to. Because she's not worried.

First and most important: The royal smile. The royal smile is neither too enthusiastic nor too bored. It gives away nothing. The top set of teeth should be on display, resting gently on your lower lip. (That is why it is dangerous to eat leafy vegetables in public.) The key is to focus on lifting your cheek muscles, not widening your mouth. As with most everything in life, Madame Vidya explained, practise enough and muscle memory will take over.

Second: Always be slightly more gracious than people expect. Be generous, especially because so often it will cost you nothing. Remember a key detail; give an unusual compliment. This will help your subjects see you as human. Practise enough and muscle memory will take over.

Third: Always be slightly more distant than people want. You can love things – chocolate treats, dried sunapples, your auntie Nithya – and you can hate things – snort-hog sausages, the Hesketh boys, your father's Hounds that aren't actually hounds at all – but love them and hate them privately. If someone gives you a gift or a kindness, act appreciative but not indebted. Crisp pronunciation, perfect posture and a handy royal smile will also help your subjects see you as a future ruler, as opposed to a sunapple-snarfing yak-oose. (OK, the Princess added that bit.) Practise enough and muscle memory will take over.

Fourth: Questions with questions. Any time you're asked a question you'd rather not answer, simply ask a question back. All the better if it invites the other person to talk about themselves. People Love to Talk About Themselves So Let Them. (Madame Vidya did in fact have the Princess write that with capital letters.) Practise it enough and ... see?

4

The Princess

A CUNNING ENCOUNTER

The foot was at the Boundary Mists, so that is where the Princess is. It's always been said that the Mists surrounding the Kingdom are what keep the people of Mistmir safe. But that assumes you're inside the Kingdom and want to stay there. The Mists themselves have never been safe. If you somehow make it through their solid surface, you could disappear forever. Even now, their swirl hints at shadows lurking beyond.

The Princess forces herself to look away and start digging, using the ten-more strategy. Every day, she sifts through the Snow in sets of ten shovelfuls, searching for something, anything that will let her say the words *Father, I have something to show you.* Every time she wants to stop, she reminds herself: she isn't going to get her kingdom back with what she doesn't find, but with what she does.

But as her back warms and her shadow shrinks, yet again she has found precisely nothing. She can feel the disappointment creeping in. That's what she gets for hoping. Already this day feels like a waste.

But then again, a waste of what? A day? She lacks many things, but she has days in abundance. Days and Snow.

Time for ten more. One, two, three, four, five—

The milky swirl of the Mists seems to whisper to her, inviting her to the Beyond Lands. It must be a trick of the light, and yet the Princess can't help but reach toward the Mists' surface with her gloved hand.

The Mists seem to whirr—

But ... the Mists don't whirr.

The King's Hounds do.

The Princess freezes, hand midair. She takes a careful step backwards. By the time she turns, the Hound is already slowing its approach. This is what she gets for letting herself be distracted.

It's Cunning, the leader of the King's pack. The Princess considers it the thinker, not because it's smart, exactly, but because it's the lead dog and lacks some of the more vicious features – the razor claws, the oversized fangs – of the others the King built. But that doesn't mean it's harmless. The Princess has seen Cunning attack. Were it to attack now the rest of the pack would zoom to this spot to join it. Or so she's been told.

Foot-runners down, Cunning glides nearer to her, stopping three arm's-lengths away. It tilts its head up and down, its two eye-like orbs lighting up red as they scan and sense her. It extends all four legs so it is standing. It's been trained to recognize her, and yet it can never just ignore her and move on. In moments like these, it feels like Mistmir is more the Hounds' kingdom than her own.

Clomp. Clomp. Clomp.

It steps toward her.

She knows the routine. Inspect, circle, leave. Find another part of the Kingdom to curse with its presence.

The Princess holds her breath as it marches around her, flattening its path as it approaches the Mists. It too knows to avoid them.

Cunning stops in front of her. The Princess exhales as she waits for it to go.

Instead, it takes another step forward. Two arm's-lengths away.

What is going on? It's supposed to know her. It's supposed to leave. Is it confused by the extra tools on her back? Or is it distracted by the Mists?

Her mind flicks back to last night, the foot, the hand. *Please don't come back now.*

Could Cunning know? But that's ridiculous. It's a machine. Still, were the person to come through now, what would happen? There's no question. Cunning would see them as an enemy. It would attack. It's a Hound. That's what it's been trained to do. Then it would report the find to the King. But the Stranger isn't Cunning's find. They're the Princess's.

Please, please, please don't come back now.

Cunning faces her again. It's close enough that, were it alive, she would be able to smell its foul breath. Of course, were it alive, she'd toss it a treat and send it on its way. She tightens her grip on her shovel. She could swing it if she had to.

Cunning settles back down on its runners, the position for speed in the Snow. The Princess readies her arms.

Cunning turns sharply away. It's done with this section of the Kingdom. The Princess stares at the shovel in her hands. She has the rest of the day to dig ten more and ten more and ten more in this spot, Hound free.

Somehow, that should feel like more of a relief.

The Princess's throat tightens as she starts shovelling again. The colours from the sunrise are long gone, and the Snow is pure white. Every shovelful, white after white after white. Just as it's always been, just as it will always be. There's no sign of anything from last night or ever. Ten more, she tells herself, but why? She could stop at seven, or eight or nine.

But she can't. Her arms won't let her. Muscle memory and all that. So she goes to ten, subjecting herself to white, white, white, green—

Green?

Green!

Of all the colours the Snow can be, green is not one. The Princess blinks a few times to be certain the sun isn't making her see spots. But no, peeking out from the snow is a small patch of fabric the colour of spring grass.

The Princess holds absolutely still. Silence surrounds her. Even the Snow, all filled in, doesn't make a sound.

Very carefully she shakes the shovel again. More flakes fall away, revealing more green fabric, this bit the colour of forest ferns. It takes all her discipline and, yes, etiquette training to freeze her muscles. Except her heart. There's not much she can do about its pounding. She purses her lips and blows off the last layer of Snowflakes to see just what she'd hoped for – the dark-holly edge of a fabric wing.

Her flutterbye.

Of all the objects she could have found, this is the most precious.

The Princess inches her hands down the shovel and lets herself inhale. The Snow smells so clean it almost stings. The shovel handle seems to vibrate; she's not sure if it's because she is trembling or the flutterbye is. She clutches the handle harder. She tries not to think about the look on the King's face when she shows it to him. The shock. The joy. The pride. It's been so long. Her subjects will return, and maybe ... others too. The Princess might never have to dig again. She could be living a new life tomorrow.

This is the moment time stopped standing still. The Princess's lips spread into not a royal smile but a real one. The sensation is almost unfamiliar.

"Omigod! It'sreallyyou!"

The voice of another person, loud and alive, breaks through the air.

The Princess jumps. She spins around, startled.

In the time it takes to blink, she already knows. Her arms jiggled. Her shovel shook. It's empty now. Yes, she realizes exactly what this means, and yet she is still stunned to see the last edge of the green flutterbye – the key to her future, the end to her seemingly endless punishment – swallowed back up by the Snow.

Part Two

Ela and the Snow

5

Ela

THE FAILING-EST FAIL

Ela found the girl from the *Snow Princess* book. In other words, the actual Snow Princess. This should be a major success, right? But somehow she's failed royally. She's not sure how, exactly, since she only said six words, but the Snow Princess is staring at her like Ela just squirted ketchup on purpose on her lovely white coat.

"Uh, sorry," Ela says, even though she doesn't actually know what she is sorry for.

The Snow Princess flings her shovel. "You startled me!"

Before Ela can respond, the Snow Princess drops to her knees and starts furiously scooping snow. Holes appear with every handful, but the snow on the ground quickly shifts to fill them in just like it did with Ela's footprints last night. It's spreading over the shovel now too.

Ela picks the shovel up before it gets buried and offers it to the Snow Princess without a word. Words haven't been working so well for Ela lately.

The Snow Princess gets to her feet and blinks a few times. She straightens to her full height and dusts herself off.

"Thank you very much. Please pardon my initial reaction," she says, taking the shovel. Her voice is crisp and eerily calm, and her accent is vaguely familiar. She takes a second to not very subtly size Ela up. It feels pretty much the same as when Ela walks into the cafeteria at lunch and kids look her over to decide whether to make room for her at their tables. They don't, and it's pretty clear the Snow Princess wouldn't either.

"Are you a stranger?" she says. Her eyes are resting on Ela's too-teal snowshoes. Ela fights back the impulse to tell her the colour looked different online.

"A what?" asks Ela.

"Are you from this kingdom? Or have you spent time here?"

Ela shakes her head.

"Have we met before?"

"In person? I don't think so," says Ela.

Before she can say more, the Princess glances again at Ela's snowshoes. "Nor do I. How exactly did you get here?"

"I just went for a walk, and this is where I ended up."

The Princess narrows her eyes. "You just happened to end up here? There weren't mists?"

"It did get misty, yeah. But I kept walking and here I am." Ela gets the clear impression that her story is somehow disappointing, even though it's true.

"An accident, then. It's been known to happen." The Princess nods to herself and begins digging again. The snow whistles with each shovelful and then promptly fills each hole up.

Ela's quirky scientist parents have always taught her that all sorts of things exist that we would never imagine. Like states of matter: scientists have created condensates where all the atoms act like they're just one big atom and fluids that will spin forever once stirred. Ela's dad calls substances like that "bosie-doodle", after a famous Indian scientist named Satyendra Nath Bose. This ... this ... stuff is completely bosie-doodle too. Yet it's just as real as all the other unexpected states of matter. And so, somehow, is the Snow Princess. The one from her mother's book!

Ela wants to ask her how *she* can be real ... but that would probably earn her another death glare. Maybe it's better to start with the bosie-doodle snow.

"Does it always do this?" asks Ela. She turns in a circle. The snow is everywhere, as far as she can see. Usually the bosie-pants states of matter (not their actual scientific name) are created in a lab under the strictest conditions and don't even last a second.

"It's Snow with a capital S. And it does now," says the

Princess. For a second, her eyes rest on Ela again. "You're certain you've never seen it before?"

"I would definitely remember this stuff. Is it man-made?"

"I beg your pardon. Are you asking if men made the Snow? Do men make the Snow where you are from?"

"No. Well, maybe on ski slopes. I mean, people, not just men. It's just... Has it been like this for a while?" asks Ela.

"I would say yes, for quite some time."

"That's cool," Ela says. She gulps. The "Snow" is "cool". She has got to stop talking.

"Well, if there's nothing else, I should return to work. If you're able, try not to startle me again." With a tight smile, the Princess turns her back to Ela and starts shovelling in a different spot.

Ela nods slowly. She thinks about checking the time on her phone but doesn't. There's no need to confirm the fact that after finding the girl from the Book – the person she has been wondering about for pretty much her whole life – she was brushed off in approximately two minutes.

In a day full of fails, this is the failing-est fail of them all.

6

Ela

THE TOP FIVE FAILS OF THE PAST TWENTY-FOUR HOURS

In honour of Ela's five states of matter – solid, liquid, gas, plasma and bosie-pants – here is a countdown of Ela's top five fails of the past twenty-four hours. Yes, *five*. That number is even more remarkable because she was asleep for nine of those hours, which means she has averaged one major fail every three hours. Other kids might go three weeks or even three months without a major fail. Her ex-best friend Kavi can easily go a year without one. But for Ela, it has been quite a day.

Fail Number Five: The Vacation Fail. Yesterday, as they were packing to leave, she tried and failed to convince her parents to go on a warm, beachy vacation or even an educational city vacation. Instead, they ended up at yet another snowy cabin in some misty woods without even a pizza place for miles around. In fairness to her parents, they are hydrologists who study snow and mist, they loooove to cross-country ski, and they bring bags upon bags of their own food to cook whenever they go on one of these snow vacations. In fairness to Ela, people are meant to be warm, she's the one person in her family who doesn't ski, and who wants to eat the same food on vacation as they do at home?

Fail Number Four: The Book Fail. While her parents were bringing in the suitcases, Ela found the Book in the boot of the car, wedged between the cooler and two shopping bags. The Book! Before anyone could see, Ela sneaked it under her jacket, grabbed a paperclip off some of her mom's boring work papers, raced inside, and shut herself in the bathroom. Her plan was to unlock the Book and read for as long as she could before anyone caught her. Except no matter what angle she tried, the paperclip would not unlock the Book. She then looked in her mom's toiletries case, where she found the usual stuff and ... the beautiful green toy butterfly that her mom guards almost as closely as the Book. Ela slipped the butterfly into her jacket pocket and then attempted to open the Book with every other sharp metal object she could find – her mom's tweezers, the pointed end of the nail clippers. She was so absorbed in the task, she didn't hear her little brother at the door. He tried to open it, she yelped, and her mom came to check on them. In fairness to her brother, the cabin only has one bathroom, and he claimed he really had to go. In fairness to her, she was in the bathroom. You don't walk in on people in the bathroom! Anyway, her mother caught Ela with the Book and freaked out. Cue enormous argument. (Can an argument be enormous but also boring and repetitive? Ela thinks yes.) The only reason this doesn't count as multiple fails is that Ela did get the green butterfly.

Fail Number Three: The Vertigsnow Fail. After the fight with her mom, Ela needed a break from everyone. She strapped on her snowshoes and took off on the nearest path into the woods. The moon on the pine trees cast long arrow-shaped shadows, pointing her deeper into the woods, toward a gauzy mist. Soon, she'd forgotten about the argument, the Book, about everything but the strange and beautiful woods.

Then the dizziness slammed her. Everything began to sway. The only reason she didn't fall down is that she slumped against a tree, which propped her up. When you get vertigsnow – that's what her dad calls it when she gets dizzy in the snow – for the first time in years, that's a fail. When a tree turns out to be more coordinated than you are, that is a fail and a half. (Still, contrary to what she has learned in maths class, she is rounding down and only counting this as one fail.)

Fail Number Two: The Run-Away Fail. And then Ela found *her*. Through the mist, she saw the girl from the cover of the *Snow Princess* book. The girl she's been curious about for pretty much her whole life. And what did Ela do when she recovered? Say hello? Ask her name? Introduce herself? Uh, no, no and no. Ela ran away as fast as she could in snowshoes.

Fail Number One: The Snow Princess Hates Me Fail. Ela thought she was so brave coming back here this morning after her parents and Akash had left for skiing. Ela thought she'd find the Snow Princess, who would then graciously answer all her questions. Ela thought those things, but now she thinks she should probably stop thinking. Because the Snow Princess clearly wants nothing to do with her.

Ela would just shuffle back through the mist and woods to the cabin except for two things: First, it is impossible to shuffle through this bosie-doodle Snow in her snowshoes. Second, she has had more than enough fails for one day.

7

Ela

ONCE UPON A TIME

Once upon a time, Ela's mother would read her the *Snow Princess* book every night and, if Ela asked, even during the day. As Ela listened, snuggled close to her mother, she would trace the fancy letters with her finger, help turn the thick pages, and fidget with the Book's shiny open latch. Her mother's voice would transport her to a hidden kingdom with elabourate parties and the most delicious jams for breakfast, and Ela's mind would drift to a place of wonder or, if it were late enough, dreamy sleep.

One evening, when her mother was busy with her baby brother, Ela went to her parents' room to get the Book. It had been a particularly bewildering day at school, and Ela was ready to smell the Book's faint rose-garden scent and rub her fingers on the curve of the "S" in the embossed title until her mom was ready to read. Only, when Ela searched for the Book on its usual shelf, it wasn't there. Nor was it on the shelf above or below or on her parents' nightstands or dresser. It wasn't even under their bed.

She looked again at the bookshelf. That's when she noticed, on the top shelf, a messy stack of her parents' science books. This was strange, because her parents liked to keep their books neat, especially if they were about science. Stranger still was the familiar corner of leather sticking out from the bottom of the pile.

Ela couldn't imagine what the Book was doing up there. It had to be a mistake. She pushed one of the comfy chairs toward the bookshelf and climbed onto it. Her feet sank into the seat cushion, and she wobbled a bit, but she was tall enough now. She tugged at the Book's cover.

THUD! Thud-thud-thud!

Ela came crashing to the floor, along with a heap of books.

Ela sat up, stunned but not hurt. The *Snow Princess* book was next to her, open to an unfamiliar page, with a different kind of writing and only one sentence. She recognized one word: E-L-A. Her name. She'd have to sound out the rest.

Her mother rushed into the room. "Are you OK? What happened, Ela?"

"The Book was in the wrong place."

"The Book?" Ela's mom spotted it on the floor. She swept it up. "Ela! It's not... You're supposed to stay safe."

Ela stared at the space on the carpet where the Book had just been.

"Ela, you know you're not supposed to climb like that." Her mother sighed. "I think our days of reading the Book are over."

"Over?"

"Yes, over... You're getting so big. Maybe we should be reading more books to help you learn to read, like the Frog and Toad ones or the Owl and Mouse ones."

"But I like this book best of all." Ela wanted to cry. If she'd been good at climbing things like the girl Harper in her class or good at reading like her tablemate Kavi, none of this would have happened. "My name was in the Book. I saw it."

Her mom's eyes opened wide, and Ela was scared she might yell. Instead, she whispered, "What else did you see?"

"Nothing," mumbled Ela.

"Nothing is good." Her mom retreated to her wardrobe.

By the time Ela followed her into the closet, she was holding a key so fancy it looked like jewellery.

"Mommy?"

Her mother didn't even look at her. Instead, she snapped the latch shut and turned the key. In an instant, the Book was locked.

When Ela searched for the Book in the weeks and months after, it was as if she'd imagined the whole thing.

As if the Book with her name in it that smelled like roses had never existed at all. When she got older, she did see it again. She'd catch her parents reading it with anxious whispers or occasionally find where it was hidden. But she could never open it. The only clue to the barely remembered story inside was the eerily realistic drawing of the Snow Princess on the cover, staring back out at her.

8

Ela

THE WORST STORY EVER

"Can I help you dig or whatever?" Ela asks the Snow Princess now. Her dad always says if you make yourself useful, people will let you stay despite themselves. Ela still has not figured out what it means to be useful in, say, the middle school cafeteria or to her ex-best friend, Kavi Bhatt. But this might be the one thing that's easier in the land of Snow.

Or maybe not. For a split second, a look of horror crosses the Snow Princess's face. But then she smiles prettily. "Isn't there something else you'd rather do? I'd hate to trouble you."

"All I want to do is help," says Ela.

"Well" – the Princess glances down at the smooth Snow – "I suppose that would be all right. For a few minutes." Her smile is as fixed as superglue on hair.

"Great!" Ela is staying, and that matters a whole lot more than a fake smile.

"Here you go." The Snow Princess reaches behind her and pulls out a little shovel that is almost the same size and shape as the one Akash used to build sandcastles that one time they went to the beach, only this shovel is metal and wood instead of plastic.

"Um ... OK." By staying, Ela is not failing, and she is determined to keep not failing even if it means digging with the most useless snow shovel she's ever seen. "What am I looking for?"

"Anything that isn't Snow."

Ela soon realizes that *everything* here is Snow. Also, digging is harder than you'd think. She has to bend over because the shovel handle is so short, and she can make only the silliest little holes before the Snow fills them in. But maybe if she does manage to find something, the Snow Princess will start talking to her for real.

Ela tosses aside random chunks of Snow. She's pretty sure there's a bunch of spots she's dug up twice, and even more that she's missed. Meanwhile, the Princess wields her shovel like it's a chef's knife, peeling and slicing the Snow. Once, when the Princess's shovel hits the edge of the mist – the mist that Ela walked right through – it clangs like two solids hitting. Ela's about to say something, but the Princess just sidesteps away without missing a beat, as if rock-hard mist is a perfectly normal state of matter here. Then again, it probably is.

"You're so good at that," says Ela.

The Princess smirks as she continues to churn the Snow into a cloud of silver. "I've had some practise."

Ela tries to imagine doing this for a few days, or even the rest of the day, every hole filling before you've dug the next. Who cares how pretty it is? That would be completely, mind-numbingly boring.

"This is kind of like Sisyphus, isn't it?"

"I beg your pardon?"

"You know, Sisyphus, from the Greek myths."

"Perhaps you could refresh my recollection of Sissy-wuss?"

Ela tries not to laugh but accidentally snorts instead. Sissy-wuss? That sounds like something Travis Houlton would call you if you flinched when he fake-punched you. Or maybe even if you didn't.

"Not Sissy-wuss. Sisyphus. He was the guy who had to push a boulder uphill for all eternity. As a punishment." Sometimes when her father's research isn't going well, he says he feels like Sisyphus.

The Snow Princess slows her shovel. Though her eyes are still on the Snow, for the first time since Ela arrived, she actually seems to be listening. "A punishment for what?"

"For cheating death."

"But—" The Snow Princess twitches her nose in a

weirdly familiar way. "Why in the King's name would he be punished for *that*?"

"I don't know." Ela never thought much about that part. Usually, Ela just imagines being flattened by the boulder on her first day on the job.

"It makes no sense. Wouldn't it be good to cheat death? If you thought someone might be dead and then you found proof that they weren't, wouldn't that be cause for celebration?" The Princess stabs the Snow with her shovel. "Wouldn't you say whoever lost them had earned forgiveness, not punishment?"

"It's just a—" Ela cuts herself off before she says "story". That's what her mom says about the Book, and it makes her mad every single time. "Anyway, Sisyphus was supposed to have done all this other bad stuff, so he might have deserved it after all."

The Snow Princess stares across her field of perfect Snow. "He probably did. But it's still the worst story I have ever heard."

9

Ela

FAVOURITE NUMBERS

OK, so maybe the story of Sisyphus was not the best way to start a conversation with someone who is digging Snow that refills itself. The problem is that Ela is about to burst from all the questions she can't ask: *Could you tell me everything about yourself, which might tell me something about me and why I matter? Or maybe you could just explain why my mom seems to be more interested in a book about you than the real me?*

No. She can't risk messing this up more than she already has. She reaches into her pocket for her mom's butterfly, but she can't find it. It must be under her phone. OK then. She is going to focus on digging. She tosses aside a scoopful of crooked, shifting flakes, then another and another.

Except snowflakes aren't supposed to shift. Or be crooked. They have six stable sides. At least non-bosie-doodle snowflakes do.

Ela peers at the flakes stuck to her tiny shovel and

counts. One, two, three, four, five, six ... seven? Impossible!

She counts again, but it's tricky because the exact shape of the snowflakes keeps shifting to fit the flakes around them. *The molecular structure of water is more* fluid *than people often realize.* Her father loves that pun. But this is taking it to a whole other level! She stares at the flakes. They all have seven sides, and though it is hard to tell exactly without a magnifying glass, each flake appears to be engaged in a strange dance to stay attached to its neighbours. One flake is isolated on the edge of her shovel, and it's extra wiggly, trying to reach the others.

Ela's mom taught her to make wishes on snowflakes when she was little, and Ela blows hard on the wiggly one while it's still by itself. Ela looks at the Princess and makes a wish. *I hope she'll give me the answers I'm looking for.*

As soon as she's exhaled, she has doubts – her wish feels like a stretch, considering the Princess doesn't want to talk to her at all. But her flake has already hit the ground and become a part of the seamless blanket that covers the land. Ela tries to think of something harmless to say that doesn't mention the Book, or Sisyphus, or this strange seven-sided Snow. Definitely not that.

"What's your favourite number?" blurts Ela. She bites her lip. That is sort of a question about the Snow, but hopefully the Princess won't figure that out.

"I beg your pardon? Did you say something?" The Snow

Princess glances at Ela for just a second. She digs so quickly, and the Snow fills so quickly, it seems alive, like a fast-forward video of a sea star regrowing a limb.

"Your favourite number? Do you have one? Mine is six. It's kind of overlooked. Everyone talks about being number one or a perfect ten or gives high-fives. Good things come in threes or a pair, which is two, and there's lucky seven—" Oops. Ela did not mean to mention the number seven. "Anyway, six is my favourite and not just because of sn-hexagons."

"Snexagons? Is that something to do with Sisyphus?"

"No, um, I meant to say hexagons. Six-sided things."

The blur that is the Snow Princess's shovel comes to an abrupt stop. She touches a gloved finger to the metal scooper and lifts off a single quivering flake. She purses her lips for a moment, and Ela thinks she is about to make her own Snowflake wish. But then the Snow Princess says, "Would you like to know my least favourite number?"

"Sure," says Ela.

"Seven," the Snow Princess replies, and flicks the flake to the ground.

Ela decides two things. First, the Snow Princess is a little too smart for her own good, or at least Ela's good. And second, if Ela doesn't want to fail anymore, she should give the Princess space. The mist she came through shines silver, but she doesn't go that way. Instead, she goes in the opposite direction, toward a bare white hillside almost as bright as the sky. As she walks, she thinks about the Snow Princess. The more she does, the more Ela feels like she knows her for real, not just from the Book. But that's impossible.

She can almost hear her parents reply that more is possible than most people know, and she should always keep an open mind. Then again, their advice doesn't always work out so well. Like last year when she had that science exam on the properties of water. She was so ready to finally beat her friend Kavi on a test for once, she wrote a whole paragraph on the strength of water, how over time it could carve holes in solid rock and create cave systems so long that they could even reach into other worlds – facts she's learned from her hydrologist father. Her paper came back with a comment in harsh red ink: *Impossible! NOT what we studied*. Of course it wasn't. It was way more interesting. But clearly she was the only one who thought so, because she failed. Meanwhile, Kavi got a hundred for a completely boring discussion on how one property of water is wetting, even though a three-year-old could tell you water gets things wet.

But now her parents' advice may be paying off. Because this place with this Snow and the Princess is more than possible – it's real. Ela stuffs her hand in her pocket and thinks as she reaches around her phone. She still doesn't feel the butterfly. Weird.

A yelp tears through the air. The Snow Princess's yelp.

Though her back is mostly to Ela, Ela can see she's completely still, holding her shovel at a funny angle. Ela rushes toward her as best she can, the slope of the land helping her along.

"Are you OK?" she calls.

The Snow Princess doesn't turn around as she starts fiddling with her shovel. "Did I frighten you with my outburst? Please do excuse me."

"You didn't, I mean, you did, but—?" The Snow Princess appears to dump a large snowball from the shovel into her pocket. "Why are you putting Snow in your pocket?"

The Snow Princess glances at Ela with that perfect smile painted on her face, her hand plastered protectively on her coat. "Snow in my pocket? Isn't that silly of me? Now, please, if you'll excuse me, I've somewhere I need to go."

Ela's stomach drops. The Snow Princess can't leave now, not before Ela's had a chance to learn anything. But she's already hurrying off, and even without snowshoes and with all sorts of tools strapped to her back, she moves through the Snow faster than Ela ever could.

Ela finally thinks of a question – the first one she should have asked. "But – who are you?"

The girl positively glows as she turns back to Ela. "I am officially the Princess."

Part Three

A Short Walk to the Cottage

10

The Princess

THE DOWNSIDE OF ETIQUETTE TRAINING

She will be called Princess again.

She found the flutterbye a second time – what are the chances? – and this time it's safe in her pocket, out of the Snow's smothering reach. She can almost hear the crowd cheering, the word "Princess" on their lips. Even this strange girl in her strange shoes. The joy and relief of it course through her pounding heart, her straightening back, her legs ready to make the journey to show the King.

"Uh, Princess?" says the girl.

She says it more like a name than a title. Not that the Princess would correct her. Etiquette training and all that. But really, could she be more of a Stranger? When the Princess dreamed of someone returning, she hoped for her aunt or her nanny or tutor, or even one of her subjects. Not a random person who stumbled through the Mists by accident.

"Where are you going?"

The Princess is going up the small hill to the High Plateau, where she will drop off her strap-sack at the Gardener's Cottage and perhaps eat a snack if she's able. Then she will walk past the Yurts of Plenty and up to the Royal Ridge, where she'll survey her kingdom: the city in the valley, the outlying farmlands, the Meander River that runs through it all. Then she'll hike down the Royal Slope and cross the bridge to the castle. There, she will rouse the King and show him the green flutterbye, the key to opening the Kingdom again. He'll commend her and forgive her, and she will start the next chapter of her life. In other words, she is going to get time moving again.

"Where am I going? Hmm. Do you have any thoughts on where to go now?" Questions with questions. Royal smile. Madame Vidya would be so proud.

"Anywhere warm, I guess?"

"What an excellent suggestion! Perhaps I'll stop by the Gardener's Cottage for a cup of tea." See? A bit nicer than expected. Practically muscle memory.

"Tea? That sounds so nice. It's freezing here."

"If you're cold, perhaps you should—" Go away and give the Princess some time to restore her kingdom in peace. But of course the Princess would never say that out loud.

"I'd love to join you!" says the girl.

"Join ... me? Isn't that an interesting thought?" says

the Princess, mentally cursing every last minute of her etiquette training. The last thing she needs at the moment is this Stranger complicating things.

The girl is a slow follower, but the Princess doesn't look back. There are no people, no buildings, just Snow and sky and, at the horizon, haze. Even she should be able to find her way up the hill.

"Uh, Princess." The Princess drops her pace a hair but doesn't stop. "Did you hear something?"

The Princess heard nothing, and she's quite sure the girl didn't either. Or if not nothing, simply the Snow. What else could it be? A Hound?

A Hound!

The Princess freezes.

Cunning is gone, but could another one come here? Could they know there's a Stranger in Mistmir? They couldn't ... or at least they shouldn't. But if a Hound found an actual Stranger? They've been trained to alert the King and attack. That is their purpose. The Princess could kick herself for getting so distracted.

She runs over the crest of the hill, scanning the landscape. Yurts, cottage, the Ice Marker and Snow, of course. No clomping march, no mechanical barks. She looks between the trees that frame each side of the plateau. No Hounds there either. She runs back toward the girl, who is still plodding up the small hill. Once the Princess has a chance to inspect what she found, she'll make a plan to get the girl out of Mistmir without the Hounds noticing. But for now, she'll hide her.

"What was it?" the girl asks.

The Princess forces a royal smile. "Just the Snow, it seems. But let's get to the cottage as quickly as possible. It's always a good time for tea, isn't it?"

11

Ela

VERTIGSNOW

The Princess sure is weird. For almost the entire time Ela has been in this kingdom, she thought the Princess had no interest in her, and suddenly she is the perfect host, taking her for tea. Ela shouldn't complain, though. Being in the same place is the first step to an actual conversation, right?

As they crest the hill together, buildings come into full view. There's a small grey cottage made of stone and thick glass. Its yard is surrounded by a wire-and-wood fence that is so long it disappears into the mist.

Beyond the cottage and off to the left is a round stone barn shaped like the houses Ela used to draw when she was little, until Kavi told her she was drawing them all wrong. Kavi always knew the rules. But maybe not the rules for this place. Ela would take out her phone and take a picture to show Kavi later, but she's already a little shaky. She'd probably drop her phone in the Snow. She's finally sort of stopped failing, and she doesn't want to start again now.

The Princess is a few steps ahead, with her hands in her pockets, approaching the cottage door. Ela isn't far behind, but she notices that it's getting harder and harder to walk straight. Her feet want to move at a diagonal, taking her toward the fence. Behind it, there's a person-sized, oddly-shaped block of ice – and Ela gets the strangest feeling in her chest: as if it's a magnet, pulling. She stares at it, trying to figure out what it might be, but her eyes can't seem to focus.

"Aren't you coming?" says the Princess, though her voice sounds weirdly distant. Ela's stomach is churning terribly, and the ground is spinning.

Vertigsnow.

All Ela can think is *Not here, not now.* But her insides tremble faster and harder, and spots appear before her eyes. She manages one last thought: *Please let me make it to the fence.*

But chalk up one more fail for the day, because she doesn't make it another step before she sways left, then right, then back, collapsing into the swallowing Snow.

12

Ela

A KNOWN CONDITION

Ela's first sensation when she comes to is of two surprisingly strong arms lodged under her armpits, dragging her through the Snow. Her eyes flutter open. The sun blinds her. Another wave of nausea hits her. She shuts her eyes and lets herself be pulled.

When she comes to a stop, she can feel she's in shadow from the coolness on her face. She cracks one eye open. She's at the cottage door. Its shiny black paint is peeling off, revealing layers of blue, red, white and green and in a few spots, the tan of bare wood. The most colours she's seen since she's been here.

The strong arms hoist her up and prop her against the cottage.

"Can you stand?" says the Princess.

It's only then that Ela realizes who the arms belong to.

Ela bobs her head. The Princess pushes the cottage

door open and guides Ela to a wooden bench in the entryway. The door latch clangs behind them.

Ela fumbles with the straps of her snowshoes. Once they're off, the Princess motions to a room in the back of the cottage with a narrow, unmade bed. "Please sit. Or lie down. Whatever you need. I'll be right back."

The Princess scurries off as Ela slumps on the bed, diagonally so her feet are on the floor. The room smells like campfire and mint and is mercifully dim. She peers out into the entryway, where the Princess has pairs of boots neatly lined up and bluish glass lets in light from outside. It's only after blinking a few times that Ela realizes it's actually not glass, but ice-bricks that have been moulded to fill in the holes where the stone must have fallen out.

The Princess returns a moment later with a glass of water and a plate of cookies. Her gloves are off, but her coat is still on, and the pocket where she put the Snowball is covered in a dark, wet blotch.

"Sweet on the right, savoury on the left," she says, motioning to the plate.

Ela takes a sweet cookie. It tastes a little like gingersnap, her mother's favourite kind. She nibbles. She's still woozy from collapsing.

"Are you all right?" asks the Princess.

Ela swallows. "Yeah." The cookie settles her stomach a bit.

"You're not hurt in any way?"

"Um, no. I don't think so."

"You've fully regained your faculties."

"Uh, yeah. I hope so."

"Well then, if you have recovered" – the Princess exhales and her nostrils flare – "perhaps you could explain what in the King's name *that* was all about?"

Ela picks a crumb off the cookie plate. "I don't know how to explain it."

"How can you not know? You terrified me!"

The Princess's brown skin has a pale cast to it, and her large dark eyes are full of fright. For the first time, she doesn't look like royalty at all.

"I'm really sorry. I couldn't help it," says Ela. "It was vertigsnow."

"I beg your pardon?"

"Uh, vertigsnow."

"I don't believe I'm familiar with that term."

Ela feels her face flushing. "Yeah, no one is. My dad made it up for when I get that vertigo feeling – you know: dizzy and nauseous – in the snow. It's kind of a joke." The Princess doesn't smile. Ela shrugs. "He's not as funny as he thinks he is."

The Princess raises an eyebrow. "You get unwell in the snow?"

"Sometimes. Not usually, but yeah, sometimes." Ela

rubs her finger along the chipped edge of the plate.

"And then you cannot keep your balance?" asks the Princess.

"Occasionally."

"And then you collapse altogether?" asks the Princess.

"That really has never happened before! Just this time. And I usually know before it gets too bad, and I just move away, and my parents or whoever help me. This time was the worst ever. Way worse!"

"Still, to clarify. You get dizzy and nauseous in the snow. This is a known condition."

"Yes." Seriously, the Princess should consider law school if this royalty thing doesn't work out for her.

"Then what in the King's name are you doing visiting a land of Snow? You could have gotten swallowed up and disappeared forever. It's happened before, you know." She grabs the roots of her thick black hair. For a second, she reminds Ela of her mother when she's mad.

Ela gulps. What is she doing here in a place where she so clearly doesn't belong? It's just that it doesn't seem like there's anywhere that she does.

"I wanted to talk to you," she says.

"You wanted to talk to *me*? Even though we've never met? Even though you've never set foot in Mistmir before?"

"I know it's weird. It's just that there's this book my mom has, and I think it might have something to do with me, and, I don't know, maybe if you just started talking about yourself, things might start making sense."

"Admittedly, I'm perplexed," says the Princess.

Ela's head is spinning again, and not just from the aftereffects of the vertigsnow. When she hears herself explaining why she's here, she realizes how absurd she sounds. How could the Princess help Ela understand herself when they've never met and are so completely different? So what if she's on the cover of her mom's book? Ela is a kid with not very good grades who can't find a place to sit in the cafeteria now that her ex-best friend has decided their friendship doesn't matter. The Princess is, well, a princess. And she's right. This place is too snowy for Ela, too cold and too dangerous.

"Well then," says the Princess. "If you'll excuse me, I'll make our tea, and then we'll get you to wherever you belong."

With that, she leaves Ela, who isn't sure how to explain that there doesn't seem to be anywhere she actually does belong.

Ela takes her phone out of her pocket. It's dead. She didn't expect service, but it won't even turn on. She hopes her mom doesn't text her. She gets so nervous when Ela doesn't text back right away. Ela reaches back into her pocket for the butterfly, but it's not there. She turns both pockets inside out to be sure. Nope. She hasn't had it this whole morning, then. She should go back and search the rental cabin. Her mom will be so upset if it's lost.

As she gets to her feet, she can hear the Princess in the kitchen, filling up the kettle. She takes one last look around the room. Coats hang off one set of wall hooks, gardening tools hang off another. Two doors: one cracked open that leads to a small bathroom, and a back door, locked shut. A pile of boxes, a pair of chairs, a makeshift nightstand. Open shelves with folded clothes and stacks of books. Books? Ela is going to leave. But maybe not quite yet.

Ela rummages through the stack. The books are bound similarly to her mother's *Snow Princess* book, but they're neither as large nor as fancy. The paper isn't nearly as heavy, and none are locked.

"Are you finding everything all right?" The Princess is standing in the doorway, a faintly amused smile curling her lips.

"Yes, I mean, I wasn't snoo—" Ela doesn't bother finishing the sentence, because of course she was snooping.

The Princess waves her hand, unbothered. "You're welcome to explore. I'll let you know when the tea is ready. Until then, take your time."

"Thank you." Ela will take whatever the Princess wants to give her, even if it's just time to snoop.

13

The Princess

THE SHED-ROOM BEDROOM

The Princess peers back into the doorway of her bedroom, which used to be the shed room. (Yes, they rhyme. It's almost cruel.) The girl is flipping through a science book, but what of it? The Princess truly is happy to let her have the run of the shed-room bedroom. What will she find? Some books, some clothes, some trinkets, some blankets. The dead embers of last night's fire. Nothing that would reveal anything that matters. More important, with the girl out of the way, the Princess can study the flutterbye in peace.

At least she thinks it's the flutterbye. She had to dump it in her pocket rather quickly. She takes the kettle off the stove. If she's going to have her hopes dashed, she'd prefer to have a cup of tea to comfort her.

She rinses her usual mug, then searches for another that isn't coated in dust. Finding none, she grabs the summer shirt she uses as a dish towel and wipes one down. The King may have decreed "Time shall stand still" when he ordered her to start digging, but the dust at least has carried on as if nothing happened. It returns so regularly, it could be the Snow's cousin.

She inhales to steady her shaking hands and then pours. The scent of kettle water fills her nose. When it's warmed like this, it smells like it's seeped from the earth and wants to linger. Not like just-melted Snow, which smells like it wants to escape. Ironic, since the Snow refuses to leave. Though maybe things are about to change. The Princess shuts her eyes and pulls out the wet fabric in her pocket. She peeks with one eye.

It is the flutterbye.

The last flutterbye.

14

The Princess

A RATHER EVENTFUL BIRTHDAY

What is a flutterbye?

Perhaps it's time for a story.

Once upon a time, all the flutterbyes in Mistmir belonged to the Princess. They were almost as much of her birthright as the Kingdom itself.

She received her first flutterbye on her first birthday. She obviously doesn't remember it, but if she had been a few years older, she certainly would, as it was a rather eventful one.

It was the first royal party in the Kingdom of Mistmir since the Queen – the Princess's mother – had died three seasons before. Though three seasons isn't nearly enough to mourn a kind, bright queen who died much too soon, three seasons is a long time to spend under the solid weight of grief, and most everyone seemed ready for some cheer. The castle had sprung to life. Fires blazed in the throne room's massive fireplaces, crepe-satin streamers adorned its ceilings and columns, and every surface gleamed. Musicians and mulled sweetberry wine entertained the adults; jugglers and bubbly sunapple punch entertained the children.

Between mouthfuls of fancy snacks and gossip, the guests cooed at the Princess and attempted to pinch her round cheeks. Her nanny, Amma, and her auntie Nithya took turns trying to protect her from the cheek-pinchers, bouncing her in their arms and calming her with hummed songs and soft toys. Nevertheless, the Princess was having a miserable time.

So was the King. It is never fun to watch others celebrate when you are still aching with loss. And it is said that the Queen was his one and only love before he decided he'd only love things that couldn't die on him. Yet, as the host, he was hardly in a position to leave. And as a lifelong resident of Mistmir, he knew better than to hope the party would be over soon.

For outside the castle, a blizzard raged. The first snow of the season had started as a lovely herald of winter earlier that afternoon but had turned into a full-on storm after the guests arrived. The King, like all Mistmirians, had learned at an early age that snowstorms made it especially difficult to get rid of visitors. Indeed, his subjects had refilled their cups and plates, and settled in by the roaring fire. Even the castle guards were huddled inside the entryway, warming their hands on mugs of steaming cider. Living in this climate, the people knew what they could withstand – and what they couldn't. And this wasn't a storm for even the most weather-hardened folks to brave.

It was hours after the baby Princess's bedtime when the King decided to shut everyone up the only way he knew how to politely – by giving a toast. He rose from his throne with his glass in hand. The chattering that filled the room turned to murmurs, the murmurs to silence.

"Tonight..." the King started. And then, because he'd been taught that repeating the first word of a sentence made him sound more important, he again said, "Tonight—"

This time he stopped because he heard sounds from behind him that were not the howling wind or pelting snow. But when he glanced back, all he saw were the thick dark-red curtains that hung inside the doorway to keep out the cold and other unwanteds. He turned back to the room where all his subjects waited – as he liked to point out when his sister got on his nerves, even his family were technically his subjects – and started again.

"Tonight—" This time he kept talking, but no one heard what he said because of a thunderous knock on the castle doors.

BOOM. BOOM. BOOM.

The fires spat. The crowd buzzed. The King glanced at a castle guard and gave her a hint of a nod. She pushed aside the curtains and unlatched the doors.

In stumbled six people so crusted with ice and snow, they were hardly recognizable as human.

While the party guests gasped and stared, the King stood, motionless and speechless. He didn't appreciate having his toast interrupted. But even more, he knew as well as anyone that Strangers didn't just appear in Mistmir, and especially not in winter. Even if the rivers hadn't yet frozen over, this should not have happened. His only consolation was that these Strangers seemed even more stunned than his subjects. They blinked and rubbed their eyes, and a few clutched each other's arms for support. For a moment, neither Stranger nor Mistmirian spoke.

Then the tallest Stranger said to no one in particular, "This place? You're – you're real?" His neck craned in all directions.

"I think many of us would like to ask the same of you," said the King's sister, Nithya, stepping forward with the young Princess in her arms. "Though the evidence would seem to support that you are." She glanced down at the ice melting off the Stranger's odd footwear, pooling on the silk-wool carpet, and smiled.

The few guests that chuckled were quickly cut off by Jeevan Hesketh, a respected Trader and newly appointed adviser to the King. "Strangers have breached the Mists," he said. "Before we start joking around, perhaps we should ascertain their intentions."

As Traders were the only people in Mistmir who'd had firsthand encounters with the Beyond Lands – after all, that is where they went to do their trading – his words carried considerable weight.

"Please excuse us," said the smallest Stranger, pulling back her icy hood. It was only then that the guests realized she was a woman, and an older one at that. "We are simply in need of refuge from the storm. We come in peace, seeking only knowledge. We're hydrologists."

"Water scientists," Nithya whispered to the King.

He bristled. It was one thing for her to help him in their private conferences, but quite another in front of an entire party. Besides, if his know-it-all younger sister had just given him a minute, he would have worked out what the word meant himself.

"So they say," muttered Hesketh loudly.

"They also say they need refuge, and that at least is indisputable," replied Nithya.

Indeed, they were a particularly pathetic-looking lot, dazed, dripping and still shivering uncontrollably. The lands beyond the Mists might be more advanced than Mistmir in many ways, but winter wear was not one of them.

Everyone, including the King, looked back and forth between the King's sister and his adviser. It was true, his sister understood the finer points of ruling and rarely steered him wrong. But it was also true that Hesketh, though new, was proving himself loyal and clever. The King would have loved to summon both into a side room and have them hash it out. But several guests were clearing their throats. The King realized that they were all waiting for him to speak.

"My decision…" This time the King paused not to sound more important, but to decide what his decision actually was. "My decision … is that the Strangers may have a cup of Warming Tea, and then I shall decide their fate for the night." He hoped those words would build his reputation for both strength and fairness. It was so hard to navigate between the two.

"Thank you," said the tallest Stranger.

"It's the very least we could do. No one should be out in this storm tonight," said Nithya as she guided the Strangers into the party without so much as a glance at her brother or his most trusted Trader.

"We are so grateful for your hospitality. This place is as gracious as it is beautiful," replied the tallest Stranger as he passed through the crowd, who murmured appreciatively at the compliment. Even Lord Hesketh forced a smile. He always did know how to bide his time.

The King was not entirely sure if he'd made the right decision, nor did he know what he should do once the Strangers had finished their Warming Tea. The best he could do now was restart his speech and hope the answers became obvious by the time he'd finished.

"Tonight..." he said for a fourth time, but the crowd ignored him, too busy buzzing about the Strangers.

At this point, the King was ready to throw everyone out into the storm. If his wife had been here, she'd have helped him handle the Strangers and the guests, and the baby Princess, who had been fussing all evening. But of course the Queen wasn't here and she never would be again. He might have drowned in that thought, but then he noticed what the rest of the guests already had.

The tall man – at the time just a cold wet Stranger, though his name was Neel, and the King would come to know him well – was holding a crimson cloth-and-wire toy in front of the little Princess who was now sitting in her aunt's lap. The first flutterbye the Kingdom had ever seen. In Neel's other hand was a small black box with a knob and buttons. He pressed some combination of them, and the flutterbye took off, flying about.

The crowd, including the King, gasped. The only person who did not was the Princess. For the first time all evening, she squealed with delight, a lovely, high-pitched "Ooooo!" Then she squirmed out of her auntie Nithya's arms. She crawled and grabbed at the red plaything but Neel kept the flutterbye just out of reach.

The Princess was undaunted. She pulled herself up on her aunt's chair so she was standing and reached again. Her fist found only air. She furrowed her brow and yelled her two harshest words: "No!" and "Stop!" The flutterbye danced an arm's-length away. She stomped. The flutterbye didn't move even a hair closer. At this point, the throne room was silent but for the buzz of the flutterbye and the crackling fires. All eyes were on the Princess and this strange bit of magic.

The Princess must have realized that there was only one way to claim her prize. She removed her hands from the chair. She took one, two, three steps forward and clutched. She tumbled to the ground, but in her hand was the flutterbye. She giggled with delight.

The guests burst into applause. The Strangers, having earned their keep, were offered heaped plates of food and shelter for the night. And the King, without assistance, finally delivered his toast, to the Princess: first steps, persistence, determination. Everyone could drink to that.

Perhaps if the people of Mistmir had been less charmed, they might have guessed right away that there was more to the flutterbye than met the eye. That the Strangers did not keep such technology available in case they stumbled in on a royal toddler's birthday. But a belly full of party foods and a brush with magic can make you forget to ask all the right questions.

The Strangers (though they would simply call themselves scientists, and they really had arrived in Mistmir to study the water) stayed off and on for the better part of a decade. And each year, on the Princess's birthday, they would give her a set of flutterbyes that were ever fancier and more lovely – though their real use never lay in their looks. When she received the last of her flutterbyes – a green one – on her thirteenth birthday, she had over a hundred.

Weeks later, after the last of her subjects fled, she had none.

15

The Princess

OF FLUTTERBYES AND BUTTERFLIES

The Princess holds the green flutterbye in front of her face, letting the window light it from behind. On closer look, the edges are frayed, the antennae are crooked, and the fabric, even though damp, shows lines where it's been crumpled. It's worn and old, and yet more beautiful than ever.

It hits the Princess. Right now, she could escape the Kingdom if she wanted. She could take this flutterbye and let it guide her to a passing point in the Mists and leave everything behind. Of course, wherever she ended up, she wouldn't be a princess. She'd be an ordinary girl if she survived the journey – and she might not. There are so many stories of those who left and disappeared forever. Why would the Princess even think of escape? She's being ridiculous. Especially now that she is finally in a position to regain her kingdom. To go back to how things were.

The Princess's hands shake. She should have her tea before she goes to show the King.

"Omigod! You found my butterfly!" yelps the girl, bursting into the kitchen.

The Princess jumps just like she did the first time the girl startled her. And again, the flutterbye falls away, floating to the ground.

The girl snatches it up. "Where'd you find it? Did I drop it?"

The Princess's head is hot and muddled, like it's been filled with kettle steam. Why is this girl speaking as if it's hers?

"You're familiar with this flutterbye?"

"You mean butterfly?"

But-ter-fly. The word rings a bell deep in the Princess's memory. Her fifth birthday. The presentation of the gifts. She was so excited for them then.

"Flutterbyes!" she exclaimed as she opened the box from the Strangers. There was one in each colour of the rainbow.

"They're but-ter-flies," said Uncle Neel, though he wasn't yet her uncle.

The King put a heavy hand on the Princess's shoulder. "I believe she is the Princess of this Kingdom, and I believe you are a Stranger. So if she says, 'flut-ter-bye', it's a flutterbye."

That might have been the first moment the Princess truly understood what it meant to be royalty. For even though she knew she'd made a mistake, "flutterbye" became the term used throughout Mistmir. She'd almost forgotten the word "butterfly". Until now.

"Do you not have butterflies here? Is it too cold for bugs?"

The girl is squinting at her as if a layer of mist has settled between them.

"Bugs? You mean insects? With six legs?" At the moment, Madame Vidya's questions-with-questions advice doesn't seem to be holding up so well. But the questions are real. There are insects in Mistmir, but they're tiny things with see-through wings. Nothing as glorious as flutterbyes.

"Butterflies are my favourite. I guess that's kind of boring. Maybe it's because of this one."

None of this makes sense.

"I found it. Before we even met this morning, it was here," says the Princess. She knows she should be asking more questions, giving compliments, keeping some distance, or at the very least smiling. But those things are very hard to do right now, when this Stranger is trying to steal the key to her future.

"I must have dropped it last night. I guess it was good I came back, even if it's been kind of a fail otherwise." She laughs awkwardly.

"It's lovely. May I have another look?" says the Princess.

"Uh, sure. Just for a second." The girl hands it to her.

"I know it probably seems weird that I'm making such a big deal over an old toy. But it's the only thing I have from when I was little and I lived somewhere else I can barely remember. My mom is from there and my dad met her there, but they refuse to talk about it. And I used to play with this butterfly, but then my mom decided we needed to keep it safe, and then I couldn't even do that. In fact, she doesn't know I have it. If I lost it, I'd be in so much trouble." She claps her hand to her mouth. "I'm sorry, I'll stop babbling now. It's just – it's just been a really weird morning."

"Indeed," murmurs the Princess. She's deciphering the girl's words slowly. They are very, very hard to comprehend. Questions with questions. Questions with questions. "You believe this used to belong to you?"

"It still does. Or my mom, at least." Doubt flickers in her eyes. They settle on the Princess's fist, closed tight around the flutterbye. "Can I have it back now?"

While the Princess's brain struggles, her hand complies. The flutterbye falls. The girl catches it.

"Thanks," she says. "I think I'm going to go now." She is speaking slowly and carefully, like she is afraid of the Princess but trying not to show it. It's how the Princess's subjects talked to her after the Snow came.

The girl goes to the entryway as the Princess tries to process the properties of time. The girl claims the flutterbye used to be hers. But how?

"Thanks again for everything. It was nice meeting you. Bye," she calls.

The door slams behind her.

As the clanging of the broken latch echoes in the Princess's ears, it hits her like an ice-brick.

The girl – it's Ela. It's her cousin Ela. It has to be. It's the only way her words make sense. This is Auntie Nithya's daughter, and if she's here, it means she and Auntie Nithya survived.

They weren't lost in the Mists. They didn't die along the way. They made it to the Beyond Lands. This whole time, they've been living their lives there.

And now Ela's come back. Just like the Princess has been imagining all these years.

And also not at all like the Princess imagined. She has been picturing a little girl, maybe a hand's-width taller than before, but still small and giggly and toddling toward her. Not a frizzy-haired almost-teenager with a pimple by her nose who wears her body like a dress she hasn't grown into.

But most of all, the Princess has been picturing Auntie Nithya returning too.

The Princess's insides are too hot and too cold at the same time, like she swallowed an ice cube floating in hot tea. Every day the Princess has wondered if they made it through safely. Now she knows they did. The worst thing the Princess ever did didn't have the worst possible outcome.

And yet.

If they survived, they were supposed to forgive her. But Auntie Nithya, at least, hasn't. In all this time, she didn't come back for the Princess.

The Princess steadies herself against a wall. It's all so much.

Ela is so big, so different. Could that much time have passed? Madame Vidya once said, *What is time but a measure of change?* And in Mistmir, nothing has changed. Time may not have literally stood still, but it couldn't have passed like it does in the Beyond Lands. Because the Princess can't have been digging, alone, for the amount of time it would take for Ela to have grown that much. To return on her own.

The Princess has been fixated on finding the flutterbye. But the key to her kingdom isn't a toy.

It's Ela.

Ela, who is alive and well.

And gone.

16

Ela

AN AGREEMENT WITH THE PRINCESS

There are a lot of things that Ela is not good at: getting her parents to level with her, understanding what maths word problems are actually asking, making her ex-best friend think she's still good enough to be friends with. But at this moment, Ela is feeling as if at least she's pretty good at a few things, like getting the butterfly back and confirming the Snow Princess exists. Now, if she can just get back to the rental cabin, this trip will officially not be a fail.

She holds her breath and stares straight at the horizon. She can feel a twinge of dizziness in her head, the question mark in her stomach – the first touch of vertigsnow. But as she stomps through the Snow, the silvery mist gets closer, and the spinning inside her slows to a stop. She's going to be OK.

A wail rips through the air.

"Come back! Pleeeeaase!" The words are raw and ragged. "Please come back! You can't go!"

Ela shuts her eyes. In her mind, she's plummeting through darkness. The yells get more desperate, but Ela can't stop this falling feeling. Is this a new kind of vertigsnow?

The screaming abruptly ends. Ela blinks. She's still on her feet, her snowshoes planted in the Snow. The only sound now is the whir of Snow filling in the footprints behind her. Ela looks back. The Princess is running toward her with her boots unlaced and her coat unbuttoned.

She stops just short of Ela, panting. To Ela's shock, she squeezes her hand. "Thank the King! I thought I'd lost..."

The Princess's eyes are shining and hungry as they take in Ela. Why is the Princess looking at her like that – almost like she's prey?

Then it hits Ela. The butterfly. The Princess wants it back. She never would have returned it if Ela hadn't caught her with it. But it's Ela's. Or at least her family's. She remembers pretending to fly it through the dusty sunbeams in her parents' room, her mom's hand on hers. Her mom would say, "This can take you where you want to go; this can tell you what you need to know." That was before it became off-limits like the Book. While Ela mostly thinks her mom is being ridiculous, she also understands that her mom doesn't have many things from where she grew up. Once Ela said, "I think you'd care less if you lost your phone than if you lost this butterfly," and her mom replied, "I'd care less if I lost a thousand phones."

Ela forces herself to look the Princess in the eye as she says, "You can't have the butterfly back."

"Butterfly? You mean flutterbye?" The Princess cocks her head and studies Ela's face for long enough that Ela turns away. "I didn't come back for the flutterbye. I came back for you."

A chill washes over Ela. "Me?"

"That's correct. You."

"Why me?"

"Isn't the reason obvious? Your ... vertig – snow condition? You should have an escort. For your safety." The Princess flashes Ela her bland, perfect, completely sketchy smile. Ela really thinks she's lying. But ... it is true that she did pass out in the Snow, and the Princess did save her.

"OK, thanks, I guess," says Ela. She starts moving again toward the mist, digging her snowshoes into the Snow for extra stability.

"Ah, perhaps I wasn't clear. I thought I could show you a bit more of the Kingdom, if you'd like. We could become better acquainted. I never did give you that cup of Warming Tea. I'd like to take you to my home – not the cottage, but my real home – where I could properly host you."

At the words "real home", an image of an arched doorway pops into Ela's head. There's a room ... a bedroom with a grand fireplace and a quilt embroidered with roses with pointy petals, like the flowers on the cover of the Book. It's so clear, it feels like a memory, even though that's impossible.

A few minutes ago, Ela would have given anything for a chance to be hosted by the Princess. But the Princess wasn't interested. And now she is a little too interested. Ela might even say scarily interested. Ela edges down the hill.

The Princess walks with her, easily keeping up even with her untied boots. "Earlier you mentioned a book. I'm not unfamiliar with the book I believe you are referring to, and I could share what I know while we walk if you're still interested."

Ela stumbles a bit. Of course she's interested. She studies the Princess. And for the first time in this very strange exchange, Ela thinks the Princess might actually be telling the truth.

"What do you know about it?" Ela asks.

"There's a copy in my home, where I was hoping to take you."

There's a copy in Ela's home too, just locked and hidden. "Do you also have the key?"

The Princess pauses. "Yes, I believe you'll find that there too. Of course, the issue with the Book, like any book, is that it tells only part of the story. However, I know much of what was left out. Perhaps I could tell you about that, and you could tell me about things too. Like your family. You mentioned your mother. How is she? What is she like now?"

For a moment, Ela thinks about how to explain her mom. On one hand, she's just a mom who loves her, and Ela is grateful because she knows that plenty of kids aren't so lucky. On the other, she isn't like other moms. She's not interested in taking Ela shopping or watching TV. She doesn't bug Ela about her grades. She says those things aren't important, and maybe they're not, but sometimes Ela feels like what she's really saying is that Ela's unimportant. Or at least not as important as her research or the Book. And then other times, she's weirdly overprotective, like when she insists on walking Ela to the bus stop on foggy mornings or wants Ela to text her right when she gets home.

"She's fine. She's really into her work." Ela catches herself. "Wait, do you know her?"

"Why would I know her?" says the Princess.

"Because you just asked about her," says Ela.

"Oh, so I did. It's proper etiquette. Ask after family, offer a cup of tea, maybe some snacks too; that's what we do in Mistmir."

This sounds just like her mom, who will drop whatever she's doing on her laptop to offer a cup of tea to anyone who stops by.

"So, what do you say? Will you join me, Ela?"

Ela stops so suddenly the Snow makes a little screech. "How'd you know my name?"

"Didn't you tell it to me?"

Ela really doesn't think she did. Yes, there was Sisyphus and snexagons, and the butterfly and vertigsnow, but they never really introduced themselves. Maybe it slipped out? But, looking at the Princess's twitching smirk, maybe not.

Ela forces herself to keep walking toward the mist. The Princess could not be more sus. For all Ela knows, she could even be lying about a copy of the Book being at her house.

But even if the Princess doesn't have the Book, she clearly knows *something*, maybe even a lot of *somethings*. Somethings about Ela.

Ela needs to ignore the funny feeling lingering in her stomach. She's never going to get another chance like this.

"If I go with you, I want you to answer my questions without all your twisty talk," says Ela.

"What precisely do you mean by 'twisty talk'?" The Princess blinks innocently.

"Ugh! That," says Ela.

"I beg your pardon. The way I speak is something of a habit. But I will try to be more straightforward. And if you have any doubts about what I tell you, you're welcome to read the Book when we arrive at my home. In the meantime, I would be happy to answer your questions and regale you with stories. It will be a lovely way to pass the time."

Ela crinkles her nose. "Are you being sarcastic?"

The Princess shrugs, but she is grinning. "Only a little. I think it could be quite nice, actually. It's been some time since I had a long talk with anyone."

"Yeah, for me too," murmurs Ela. The Princess looks at her curiously, but Ela isn't about to bore her with the drama of middle school. "Let's get started. Tell me a story. Your story."

Part Four

A Long Walk to the Castle

17

The Princess

A CLARIFICATION

If Ela wants a story, Ela will get a story.

But here's the secret about stories, any stories, whether or not they're in a book: all of them leave something out.

So the Princess can tell Ela about her first birthday but not her thirteenth. She can talk about her dear aunt without making her connection to Ela clear.

Indeed, this may be the strategy for the whole trip. The Princess can tell Ela that their ultimate destination is the castle without disclosing the threat of Hounds along the way. She can talk about the beauty of the Mists without mentioning that their passing points shift unpredictably. She can show Ela the city in the valley without admitting it's been deserted.

A story might be the perfect distraction to keep Ela by her side. And it's a small price to pay to get Ela to the King.

After that, he'll take care of the rest.

18

The Princess

THE STORY OF THE BOOK

"Where should I begin?" the Princess asks Ela.

Ela chews on her lip, like she used to when she was little, and looks around as if the landscape might offer up an answer. But it won't, not here. The Princess is well aware of how barren the highlands are, with just a handful of cottages and yurts, but that was by design. There was a time when this was the place to see gardens and enjoy the views, to have some quiet away from the city below. While Ela doesn't need to remember the past – in fact, it is crucial that she doesn't – it's only right that she understand that the Kingdom is far more than just the highlands.

"I should warn you, there's not much here to talk about. My home, the main city, the smaller towns, the farmlands, all of that is in the valley. The highlands were, I mean *are*, mostly used for recreation," says the Princess.

Ela nods. "Could you tell me about the Book? The one with you on the cover," she says, drifting toward the cottage grounds. The Princess stops short. It's bad enough that she took Ela there before she realized who Ela was. They cannot return.

"Absolutely not!" The Princess scurries to her other side and angles her body so she's at least blocking the view of the Ice Marker. Ela folds her arms. "I'm not walking if you're not talking."

The Princess meets her stare. Ela's forehead and nose are so much like her father's, the Princess isn't sure how she missed it this morning. And Ela's stubbornness is just like Auntie Nithya's. To think the Princess could have sent Ela back home before she realized who she was! The Princess takes a deep breath. She mustn't let her emotions get the better of her. For Ela, the cottage is simply a cottage. And the Marker nothing more than a lopsided block of ice, not a warning of where one might disappear.

"I'm so sorry; did you misunderstand me? Of course I'll talk about the Book. It's just we're not going to the cottage now. We're going to my real home. So we need to walk toward those buildings up there." The Princess points to the yurts.

Ela bites her lip again. "Is it going to take long to get there? I need to get back before my parents do. They don't know I'm out."

The Princess feels her smile falter. "Your parents. Where are they now?"

"They went out cross-country skiing. Back by the cabin where we're staying," says Ela.

"They left you on your own?"

"Yeah. Don't get me wrong, my mom can be super overprotective, especially around snow and fog, but they know how much I hate skiing. With the vertigsnow and everything, they're happy to let me drink hot chocolate and stay in, and sometimes one of them will hang out with me. But today they both felt like it was really important for their work to explore. They work on vacation. It's weird."

A tiny piece of the Princess had hoped that maybe... But no, she hasn't been forgiven yet, not by the King, not by her subjects, and clearly not by Auntie Nithya either. "I mean, you have nothing to worry about. I know all the shortcuts. We'll get you back right on schedule." It's not a lie. The Princess didn't say *whose* schedule. "In fact, let me set the pace, and we'll go even faster." She scans for Hounds but doesn't see a trace of them. "Now then, I believe you wanted to know about the *Snow Princess* book, correct?"

"That's right," says Ela. She moves slowly in the Snow, but she's no longer drifting toward the cottage.

One step at a time, the Princess reminds herself.

"The first thing to know about the Book is that there are two copies, and they were a gift to my parents on my birth." The Princess modulates her tone so it is loud enough to hear over the Snow but soft enough that Ela will want to keep close.

"How could someone write a story about you if you were just born?"

"Oh, no. The pages were blank, and then Madame Vidya – she was the Chief Scribe and also my tutor – she would write up the big events and accomplishments after they happened, and the copying paper would take care of the rest." The Princess pauses for a moment. Again, she only hears Snow, no Hounds.

"What's copying paper?"

"Don't you have copying paper where you're from?" asks the Princess. "It's paper where anything written on one page also appears on its sister sheet somewhere else. It's made from a rare type of holly-pine tree. Each pair of books comes from the same tree, and the paper works best when it's written on with ink made from the berries and gum of that tree as well. Though the best copying paper can work with any ink. Anyway, in addition to the pages being made of copying paper, the books were bound in copying board, so the cover could be updated too. Any changes from one copy of the book would transfer to the other, so each parent could know what was happening with their child even if they were apart." The Princess actually thought the Beyond Lands had a similar invention, but it can be hard to keep track.

"Wait – each of your parents has a copy of the Book?"

"Well, that is how it was supposed to be, but ... my mother died when I was very young."

"Oh, I'm so sorry!" Ela's eyebrows crease into a *V* and her lips tighten into a concerned pucker. In this moment, she so resembles the little girl the Princess once knew.

"It's all right. It was a long time ago." Amma first taught the Princess to say that when it hadn't been that long at all, and she needed to curl up with Auntie Nithya each night to fall asleep. Amma said it was the type of answer that makes the person you're talking with feel more comfortable. Not exactly a lie, but not exactly the truth.

One day the Princess asked if it was her fault her mother died. After all, many people fell ill that winter yet had recovered by the spring thaw. But her mother, who'd given birth to her just months before, was gone. Her question was met with an immediate and forceful chorus of "No!" and "Certainly not!" and "How could you ever think such a thing?" from Amma, Auntie Nithya, and Madame Vidya. They replied with such vehemence that the Princess wondered if their answers were really aimed at making her more comfortable. Again, not exactly a lie, but not exactly the truth.

"Anyway," the Princess says to Ela, "I was hardly alone. Auntie N—" The Princess catches herself before she says her aunt's full name. "My aunt and Amma, my nanny, and my tutor, Madame Vidya, all cared for me and raised me.

And my father of course." The Princess pauses. That last bit is actually mostly a lie.

But Ela accepts it without question. "That's nice, I guess, but I'm still sorry that happened to you." Her face is etched with concern.

"Thank you for saying so. I am too." Every day, in fact, usually multiple times a day, the Princess wonders how things would have been different if her mother had lived. Would her father have stayed the joyful man in his wedding portrait? Auntie Nithya used to tell the Princess stories about how naturally kind and calm the Queen always was. Could her mother have taught her how to be like that? Or would the Princess have taken her wisdom for granted? Despite all evidence to the contrary, the Princess wants to think she wouldn't have. It would be nice to have one relationship she got right.

They walk a few steps in silence, just the whine of the Snow trailing them. They're making good progress, getting close to the yurts now. Even though Ela is panting, she mostly keeps up. The Princess isn't at all sure those funny snowshoes are helping matters, but given that the Princess left the cottage so quickly, she doesn't have anything better to offer.

"Anyway, would you like to tell me about yourself? Or more about your parents?" The Princess hopes she's being subtle enough.

"My parents are … parents. My dad's a hydrologist like my mom. I guess they can be fun sometimes, but mostly they're focused on … other stuff. But anyway, let's not talk about them. Tell me what the Book says."

The Princess shouldn't have asked about Ela's parents again. She wishes she had some snacks on her; good food always makes for good distraction, as Madame Vidya liked to say. But she doesn't, so the Book will have to do. The Princess takes a deep breath.

"'The Princess was born in winter.'"

"You're the Princess you're talking about?"

"The one and only," says the Princess.

"Why don't you just say 'I', then?"

"I'm reciting the Book for you. Word for word. Although honestly, it's quite boring. Perhaps I should speed up."

"Wait, no, slow down! Do that word-for-word thing again."

The Princess sighs, but she clears her throat and continues. "'The birth was not an easy one, but as her mother laboured, the first snow of the season started to fall, and a hushed beauty covered the land. When the Princess arrived, her mother decided to name her Karina. In the Naming Language, that meant "pure" or "innocent". But her mother, who had been a scholar of languages and a translator before she became queen, knew that in other tongues "kar" meant "snow". And so, this child destined to one day rule the land, would be forever tied to the snow. She would be Mistmir's Snow Princess.'"

"Wow ... that's beautiful."

"Is it?" says the Princess, arching an eyebrow. "I suppose it's marginally better than Sissy-wuss, at least."

Ela blushes, and the Princess feels a twang of guilt. Ela is turning out to be a kind girl, and the Princess knows firsthand how unpleasant it is to be reminded of your mistakes.

The Princess suddenly realizes that she has unthinkingly mentioned her own name – the name Ela knew her by – and given a lengthy history of it. She needs to stop—

Then she hears a mechanical whirring, getting closer. Actually, they need to go. Fast.

A Hound is approaching.

She can't see it yet, but judging by the noise, it is descending from Royal Ridge. It could be here in seconds. It was built to move in snow.

The Princess glances at Ela. The girl is trudging along, happily unaware.

They need to hide.

Luckily, they are by the yurts. Unluckily, the yurts are locked. The Princess shoves her hands into her pockets and pulls out the yurt key. Never has she been more grateful for Madame Vidya's insistence that she always be prepared.

"Are you OK?" says Ela as the Princess rushes to the yurt and undoes the lock.

“Shhh. You need to get inside.”

“But you were telling me about the Book”

“Please, could you just hush and get in the yurt?”

“But—”

“Now, Ela!” the Princess says, half-pushing her in. And before Ela can say another word, the Princess slams the door shut and turns to face the creature heading straight for her.

19

Ela

THE CREATURE OUTSIDE

Maybe Ela isn't done with fails for the day. Though maybe whatever just happened doesn't count as a fail. All Ela knows for sure is that just before the door slammed shut, she heard the Snow wail and the strangest metallic scrape. And the Princess seemed scared of whatever was coming. Which probably means Ela should be terrified of it.

So maybe it's a good thing the Princess shoved her into this "yurt". Ela always thought yurts were tent-like things, but this place is more like a giant, freezing warehouse disguised as a round barn. Most of the windows are blocked by stacks of stuff, though at the very top of the roof is a skylight that lets a pool of sunlight into the centre of the yurt. Wooden beams fan out from the skylight like sun rays, and a huge spiral ramp lined with boxes, sacks and shelves circles the inside of the yurt, rising from the floor all the way to the top of the building, several storeys up. It looks like a space that could be featured on a home-restoration show – if it had heat. Ela's breath forms a wispy cloud in the dimness.

She takes off her snowshoes and starts climbing the spiral ramp. As she walks, her stomach sinks. Even if it's not her fault she's in this yurt, Ela realizes she did seriously mess up. She revealed that her mom had the *Snow Princess* book, and it turns out there are only two copies. And her mom has one of them … how, exactly? It's not as if she hangs out with royalty; she barely socializes with the neighbourhood moms. And even if she did, how would the Book end up in their house? Would her mom have … taken it without asking? She's the last person Ela would expect to steal. She's such a rule follower, she won't take more than nine items to the ten-items-or-less express checkout, "Just to be on the safe side." The whole situation is seriously sketchy. Maybe it's not the worst thing that something came to distract the Princess. Although, given how scared she seemed, maybe it is.

The door creaks open. Ela jumps.

"Are you finding any snacks to your liking?"

Though the Princess is in shadow, Ela can almost hear the polite smile through her words.

Snacks? What is up with this girl?

"I haven't been looking for snacks," says Ela.

"Well, you ought to be. The Yurts of Plenty have everything you could want. I can give you a tour if you'd like. Up at the top are everyday goods, like soap and such.

Below that are preserved foods from Mistmir; you know – pickled vegetables, hare jerky, dried fish, fruit jams, and sacks of flour. It's important to have a well-balanced diet no matter what the season. But we also have a wonderful selection of snacks. I could even get you treats from the royal stores if you'd like, though truth be told, I prefer many of the common ones. And then at the ground level is miscellaneous stuff – old equipment, metal scraps, and the like. Anyway, what are you in the mood for?"

Ela doesn't want to be rude, but really? "I am in the mood to know what the heck was outside."

"Outside?" repeats the Princess. Ela would guess the Princess is blinking innocently and smiling her perfect princess smile. Ela's glad she can't see her or she might scream.

"Yes, outside, when like a minute ago you begged me to be quiet and pushed me in here because something was coming."

"I don't beg!" says the Princess. "I asked. With a rather urgent tone, to be sure, but that's not *begging*."

"Fine, whatever. What was outside?" says Ela, making her way back down the ramp.

"Ah, yes. Well, there's the Snow, and a few yurts, and once you go into the valley, quite a lot of everything."

Ela tries to walk around the Princess to peek outside, but the Princess backs up against the door. Her sigh fills the open room. "I'll tell you. It was Cunning."

"*What* was cunning?"

"No, its name is Cunning. It's one of my father's Hounds."

"Hounds? Like a dog? You didn't want me to see a dog?"

"I didn't want the dog to see you. My father's Hounds aren't always very friendly, especially with Str— creatures they're not familiar with, so I thought it best I send it on its way."

"What do you mean 'not very friendly'? Do they bite?"

The Princess presses her lips together. "They're capable of it. To be clear, I don't know with absolute certainty that it would bite you. It might not. But why take the risk?"

Huh. Ela is pretty sure this is, as her dad would say, not what she signed up for. "Why didn't you tell me about the Hounds when we first started walking?"

"Because there aren't that many for the size of our Kingdom. There are days when I don't encounter them at all."

"How many are there?"

"Eight or so? Which for a Kingdom this size is quite few."

"And one is called *Cunning*?" Ela shivers – because the yurt is freezing, but also because that's a creepy name for a dog. "What are the others named?"

"Oh, it's hard to remember them all," says the Princess, waving airily. "After all, the King named them, not me. Anyway, take a look around the yurt. You're sure to find something delightful."

20

The Princess

THE HOUNDS' NAMES

First of all, eight does round up to ten, which is how many Hounds there are if you're counting exactly. Ten Hounds with ten names: Cunning, Cutter, Bruising, Biter, Ranging, Ripper, Piercing, Pouncer, Menacing, Mauler. Each a gift from the Strangers, though of course they didn't give them to the King in their current form. The King did that part all himself.

The Princess often thinks it was quite cunning of the King to start with Cunning as the first name. If the King had started with, say, Ripper or Biter, the Strangers would have likely said, "It's been nice; I think we'll take our doggie-sleds back now."

But they didn't, and they let him keep ten in total before they realized their mistake. Because once the King turned them from doggie-sleds to Hounds, the Strangers became their first target.

The Princess isn't lying when she says she's not exactly

sure what they'd do if they saw Ela. It's true the Princess has seen them attack, and it's true that the King claimed their purpose was to protect the Kingdom from Strangers. But the Princess has never asked how they've been trained for a situation like this, with someone just wandering in.

The point is, she's going to keep Ela safe. But she doesn't need to delve into the details about the Hounds to do that. If anything, that will scare Ela, which will slow things down, and that is in neither of their interests. For now, she just needs Ela to stay positive. Or distracted, at least.

The Princess forces some enthusiasm into her voice. "So, I'm going to gather us up some delicious snacks for the rest of our walk. Why don't you look around for anything else that might interest you here? And if you'd like, I could tell you another story. In fact, I have one about this very yurt. Shall I tell it?"

"Sure, I guess so," says Ela, already rummaging through boxes.

This girl's curiosity is a gift. To the Princess, at least.

21

The Princess

THE YURT STORY THE PRINCESS TELLS

The Yurts of Plenty were a symbol of all that was right about Mistmir. The Mists, by and large, kept its citizens safe from outside threats. The yurts ensured they were well nourished. Beyond being safe and fed, what else could a subject ask for? The rest would fall into place. (This turned out not to be entirely true, but the Princess learned that long after this story happened.)

There were two ways Mistmir obtained food for its citizens. The first was through its fishermen and farmers. Though the growing season was short, the soils in the valley were rich, and the crops perfectly adapted to the climate. The second way was through trade with the Beyond Lands. On the first day of summer, the Traders would depart with ships filled with Mistmir's finest goods. By autumn, they'd (hopefully) return, though with what was always a surprise. Even the Traders couldn't predict exactly where in the

Beyond Lands the water would take them, or what they'd come back with, or if they'd come back at all. There were ships that never did.

That's why the Yurts of Plenty were so important. If the Traders brought back a hefty haul and the farmers grew an abundant harvest, the excess food could be preserved and packaged to last for years and then stored in the yurts. If the Traders' ventures failed or the harvest was meagre, the King could open the yurts, and food would be distributed throughout the long winter to whoever needed it. Sometimes, during holidays or after a particularly harsh blizzard, a box of sugar candy or a bottle of blue-birch syrup would be added to the food sack to cheer things up. The key was that no one ever went hungry, and everyone was treated with respect regardless of their needs. As the Princess's aunt would say, what's the point of having power if you can't fulfill the basic needs of your people? The yurts made sure that Mistmir could.

Which is why stealing from the yurts was the equivalent of stealing from every person in the Kingdom. It was one of the gravest crimes in Mistmir.

The day the Princess found thieves in the yurt, she was not yet nine years old. The trading ships had been back safely for weeks, and their bounty was in the process of being stored away. It was late afternoon, and Amma had taken the Princess out for a walk – really more of a hike –

up the Royal Slope, the steepest way from the valley to the Royal Ridge and High Plateau. The Princess had been told many times that princesses were expected to have a strong mind and a strong body. And she did. She pulled ahead of Amma, eager for some exercise after a long day of lessons.

She reached the Royal Ridge and hiked onward, the early-autumn breeze invigorating her. But when she passed this Yurt of Plenty, she stopped and turned around. The door was cracked open.

The Princess knew that one day it would be her job to ensure that the needs of her citizens were met, and she already took that responsibility seriously. When she got close enough to the entrance to feel the yurt's cool air leaking out, she heard voices. Kid voices. The Princess slipped inside.

All three Hesketh boys were raiding the candy section! The littlest one, Jeremy, was drinking blue-birch syrup straight from the bottle. Thick drips streamed down his chin. The middle boy, Joey, who was about the Princess's age, had two jelly-spheres stuffed in his mouth, much like a chip-monkey preparing for winter. And the oldest, John, who was already a teenager – certainly old enough to know better – had his grubby hands in a bag of chocolates bearing the royal seal. None of them noticed her.

"Stop it!" cried the Princess. "You are breaking the law! The food belongs to the whole Kingdom."

Jeremy clapped his sticky hands to his sticky face.

Joey dropped the box of jelly-spheres.

John didn't even blink. "I took mine from the section reserved for royalty. So actually I'm stealing just from you." He stuffed a handful of the King's favourite chocolate drops into his mouth and chewed loudly as he walked down the ramp to the Princess. "And you can't stop me." He burped in her face.

The Princess didn't flinch. She'd made more trips out to the farmlands than she could count, visiting yak-cow barns and snort-hog stalls with a royal smile on her face. She'd even helped shovel yak-oose manure once. She knew how to handle bad smells. And she knew the boys had to behave for the same reason she always had to. "It doesn't matter if I stop you. It will go in your book, and everyone will know anyway."

At this John laughed and laughed and laughed. It lasted so long, the Princess knew he must be faking it. "We don't have books," he said.

"I have books. I read them each night before bed," said Joey, who had finally swallowed enough of his jelly-spheres to speak.

"Not that kind of book, dummy. She means the one Dad told us about, a book about your life, where things about you are written down. We're not important enough to have them. But the Princess is. She's royalty." He said the last word in a singsong voice.

No one had ever told the Princess that she was the only child with a book. It seemed like someone really should have. But then she realized that didn't matter right now – this event in the yurt was happening to her as well as the Heskeths.

"Then it will go in my book," she said triumphantly.

"Every single thing that ever happens to you isn't written about. Get over yourself." John turned back to his brothers. "Keep eating. Don't listen to her. She's just a stupid girl."

The Princess felt her jaw drop. Her hands had balled into trembling fists. No one ever spoke to the Princess like that. Never, ever.

"What?" John smirked. "The brilliant little princess can't think of her words. Poor baby. Guess you're not as smart as they say."

Oh, the Princess could think of words. Two words in particular.

"Shut up! Shut up! Shut up!" she started yelling, which was Absolutely Not Allowed. "Shut up! Shut up!"

John started yelling back, and then Jeremy dropped the syrup bottle, which shattered, but luckily not too close to anyone, and then, as the Princess was weighing whether to punch John, Lord Hesketh walked in the door.

"Children! Behave or I'll tell your mother how you've been acting."

"See? You do have to stop!" said the Princess, satisfied.

It was only right that justice would be served. Her hands relaxed.

"Oh, this applies to you too, young lady," said Lord Hesketh. "I don't believe in giving special treatment based on one's title."

This was especially rich coming from someone who had petitioned her father so he could be call "Lord".

"You can't tell my mother how I've been acting. She's dead." In that moment, the Princess didn't care one whit about making people uncomfortable. Or rather, she hoped she would.

"Ah yes, the poor little motherless princess who has the whole Kingdom wrapped around her finger." He yawned. "The tale has become rather tedious."

How dare he! What an awful man! The Princess might have said as much (even if she wasn't sure what "tedious" meant), but at that very moment she noticed the key ring in Lord Hesketh's hand. He had been the one to unlock the yurt! He had let his sons steal from the Kingdom! He was only mad because they'd been caught.

The Princess looked into his cold, dead-fish eyes. "I'm telling my father."

Lord Hesketh shrugged. "If you must." Then he collected his boys, letting them leave with the bottles and bags they'd opened. John even took a few they hadn't.

❄ ❄ ❄

"I hate them!" the Princess said to Amma as she stomped her way to the Royal Ridge.

Amma didn't have to ask who. She'd seen the Heskeths depart with their bounty. "Yes, well. It's a shame the way they're acting. But remember, you're the Princess, so it's your job to be nice." She never was as good at teaching etiquette as Madame Vidya. "I have to say, the middle one, Joey, he's not so bad."

It was true that Joey Hesketh was not as horrid as his brothers, rather the way milk that had been left out overnight was not quite as horrid as milk that had been left out for three days or four. But really, who wanted to be near any spoiled milk at all?

22

The Princess

THE YURT STORY THE PRINCESS DOESN'T TELL

Though the Princess doesn't tell it to Ela, the worst (and best) part of the story was what happened not inside the yurt, but after. Upon entering the castle, she rushed to find the King and told him what had transpired. She was ready for her father to praise her for her loyalty to the Kingdom, her dedication to upholding the common good. But most of all, she was ready for the Hesketh to get what they deserved.

Halfway through the story, the King cut her off. "Really, Karina, such a fuss over some candies?"

"But Father," said the Princess, certain that she just hadn't been clear enough, "he had the key ring with the yurt key *in his hand*—"

"Lord Hesketh is my trusted adviser and, as you well know, the lead Trader in the Kingdom. I won't hear a child, even you, speak against him, especially over a petty grievance."

Her father's rebuke stung like a slap. She knew as Princess she shouldn't cry, but sometimes, when she was very, very angry, the tears spilled out anyway. As she ran from the King's rooms and down the hall, she swore she'd never speak to anyone ever again. That promise lasted only as long as it took to find her aunt, Amma, and Madame Vidya in the small dining room, chatting before supper. The whole story spilled out.

"Why does he care so much about a stupid *Trader*?" The Princess sniffed.

"Because Hesketh is so very..." Auntie Nithya paused with a funny look on her face. Then she let out a long, rolling, massive burp. The kind that felt like it could shake furniture.

"Nithya! Etiquette!" said Madame Vidya.

Auntie Nithya shrugged. "What? Even royalty burps sometimes." She winked at the Princess, who'd instantly stopped crying. "But if you'd rather, I'm perfectly capable of complimenting Hesketh, as I have the joy of dealing with him at every royal council meeting. He's an excellent flatterer who knows how to get the King on his side, and he's very skilled at pushing the interests of what he cares most about ... which of course is himself."

"Now, now," said Madame Vidya, shooting Auntie Nithya a look.

"Please excuse me. All I meant to say was that I empathize, Kiri," said Auntie Nithya.

The Princess pinned her stare on Madame Vidya. "If I ever acted like the Hesketh, you'd make me do double etiquette lessons."

It might not have been entirely fair to single out Madame Vidya, since no matter what she thought, she couldn't directly criticize the King or his advisers, but she could at least have let Auntie Nithya do it.

"Yes, well, Lord Hesketh is the lead Trader, and as we've studied, the Traders bring back many goods that are essential to Mistmir," said Madame Vidya.

"Their work might be essential, but their attitude isn't," muttered Auntie Nithya.

"Now, they don't all have such an attitude," said Amma. "There are some very pleasant Traders in my opinion."

"And whether they're pleasant or not, it's still dangerous work navigating the currents and the Mists. You've heard the tales of shipwrecks and boats disappearing in the Mists, lost without a trace. Even with the very best ships and the very best maps, you need luck and skill. And then, even if they make it to the Beyond Lands, there are only a few select ports where they have contacts. If no one there has use for yak-cow cheese or silk-wool rugs, it is still the Traders' responsibility not to return empty-handed. If they're able to return at all," said Madame Vidya.

"I've yet to see an empty-handed Trader," said Auntie

Nithya. "And besides, they love exploring. The things they must see!"

"People who aren't Traders have been known to pass through the Mists too," said the Princess. She turned to Madame Vidya. "Your parents did, didn't they?"

Rumour had it that Madame Vidya's parents were Strangers who had stumbled into Mistmir when seeking refuge from some undefined badness in the Beyond Lands. Once they were questioned, it was clear their heads were so full of knowledge that, Strangers or not, the old King appointed them as royal tutors. But still, Strangers were Strangers, and even though the story only proved how smart Madame Vidya's family was, it was still whispered.

"That was before I was born," said Madame Vidya stiffly. "I don't know the details." She opened her mouth as if there were more to say in her defence, but then shut it.

The Princess had never seen her tutor at a loss for words before. She wanted to apologize, but if she did, was she implying that there was something wrong with having Strangers as parents? The one person she would have asked to clarify this point of etiquette was the one she might have insulted. So instead she said, "I didn't mean to pry" – a phrase Madame Vidya had taught her just the previous week – and swallowed hard. "I'm lucky to learn from you."

"Hush, dear," said Madame Vidya. "I'm lucky to teach

you. I do believe, with your intelligence and loyalty, you will be the best ruler the Kingdom has ever seen."

"Hear, hear," said Amma.

"Whatever you choose to do, you'll be amazing," said Auntie Nithya.

The three women embraced her, and in that moment, the yurt, the stolen candies, and the King's reprimand were as far away as the Beyond Lands.

23

Ela

BOX AFTER BOX

As the Princess finishes telling her story, Ela examines what feels like her hundredth box. She is in the "miscellaneous" section of the yurt, which she thinks just means "random". According to the labels on the boxes Ela has moved into the light, were she interested, she could have found, among other things, forks, spoons, knives, ladles, plates, screws, spools of ribbon, spools of thread, spools of wire, knitting needles, sewing needles, paintbrushes, scrub brushes, hairbrushes, combs, blankets, serving trays, baking trays and boating gear. But for all that, she only managed to clear enough space to look out one window, which gave her an excellent view of ... Snow. Not even paw prints, because ... Snow.

"What happened when you told the King?" Ela asks the Princess, who is standing on the ramp above her.

"I beg your pardon? Told the King what?" The Princess sounds so surprised, Ela wonders if she forgot Ela was there.

"About the Hesketh stealing the candy? You know, the story you just told? Did the King punish them?"

"Ah yes, as I recall, he didn't have much to say."

"But..." says Ela. She eyes the label on a long, thin box. Fishing rods. Not helpful.

"Being royalty is very difficult. You don't understand the pressures," says the Princess.

"That's for sure," says Ela, carrying the rod box out toward the middle of the yurt. "I am about as far from being royalty as humanly possible."

"I sincerely doubt that."

"You know how you're a princess? I'm not just 'not a princess', I'm 'even the thought of me being a princess makes people laugh out loud'," says Ela.

That is literally true. Last year, on the bus, Harper Price said, "Sometimes I secretly think I was born a princess." Ela was so surprised to hear someone like Harper say the exact thought she'd had herself that she blurted "Me too!" Everyone burst out laughing, even Ela's supposed best friend, Kavi. At the time, Ela was so embarrassed, she didn't stop to think what it meant that her best friend had laughed along with everyone else.

"Is that so?" asks the Princess. "Perhaps you could share all of the un-princess-like ways you pass your time."

"I go to school, I come home, I like to watch cooking shows and draw, but I'm not that good at it. I think shooting baskets is fun, but not actual basketball. I have too much homework, and I hate taking tests because they're more about tricking you than seeing what you actually know. And these days..." These days it seems like if you aren't really good at something, you're nothing. But the Princess, who's good at everything, would never get that. Ela pushes aside another box. "These days, there's not much else. Told you it's boring."

"At least you're educated with your friends."

Ela shakes her head. "I'm not. My best friend moved away." That is a lie. An accidental, slipped-out, easier-than-telling-the-truth lie. But still a lie. "And everyone else..." Ela shrugs. She's not a good liar, and she's sure to get caught if she keeps going.

"They left you?"

The horror in the Princess's voice floods Ela with guilt. "No one went away-away. More like just to a different, you know, part of the cafeteria."

"A cafeteria is a type of dining hall, correct?"

"Yeah, exactly. And we don't have classes together, and then there was this horrible birthday party—"

"A horrible birthday party?" interrupts the Princess. "It sounds like there's a story here."

And of course there is.

24

Ela

SMARTIES

Until the last day they were friends, it never bothered Ela that Kavi always had her hand up, always bragged about how long the books she read were, always did her homework on playdates before she would play. That's just how she was. Even when they started middle school a few months ago and had no classes together except art because Kavi was in advanced everything, Ela didn't mind. Even when Kavi started talking nonstop about Gabi and Grace, two girls in all her advanced classes, Ela didn't mind. Even when those girls started sitting with them at lunch, monopolizing Kavi's attention and ignoring Ela, she didn't mind. At least not that much.

Kavi's birthday was at the beginning of November. Ela had been working so hard on not minding for months now, she wasn't going to mind that Gabi and Grace were going to be celebrating with them. Besides, things might be different outside of school.

They actually were for a little while. The girls went out to dinner at the Everything Diner, and it was easy to talk about the best milkshake flavours and ways to serve potatoes (strawberry and curly fries, obviously), and to watch funny videos together. It was fine, all through the cake cutting back at Kavi's house. And then Kavi brought out her bag of Halloween candy.

"We should have a group name," said Gabi as she popped a handful of M&Ms into her mouth. She wasn't looking at Ela as she spoke, but seeing as how there were only four people in the room, Ela was pretty sure she was included.

"Totally," said Grace, swallowing a scoop of Fun Dip. "But what?"

"I've got it!" said Kavi. She pulled a pastel-coloured cylinder from her candy bag. "Smarties!"

"I love that. Smarties!" said Ela.

Grace coughed so hard she got Fun Dip all over herself. Gabi hooted, displaying a mouthful of chewed-up chocolate.

"Uh, I think you actually have to be smart to be a Smartie," said Gabi.

"I'm sorry, but are you in *any* advanced classes?" said Grace.

"No," said Kavi. "She's not."

Ela froze. She wanted to not mind, just like she'd been forcing herself to do since the first day of school. But she did. She minded so much. The problem was, once you admitted one thing bothered you, suddenly you were buried under an avalanche of all the things you were only pretending were fine.

Ela ran to the bathroom and locked the door, staying there even though Kavi's mom knocked twice to see if she was OK. She didn't come out until she could breathe normally, well after she'd heard Gabi and Grace getting picked up. She had already decided she wouldn't tell her mom. She couldn't risk having her mom tell her it was no big deal, not when she felt this awful. Instead, she prepared herself for Kavi's apology. That's just how it went. Kavi would say not-so-nice things, but she would always say sorry.

Ela looked at Kavi. She hoped her eyes weren't too obviously red. Kavi looked back without saying anything.

"That was really, really mean." Ela sniffed.

"Sorry, but it is kind of true," said Kavi.

That was not an apology.

"What is your problem?" Ela yelled. "You've been such a snob since school started. Harper Price is in all advanced classes too, and even she never talks about it."

"Harper is so pretty, she doesn't need to."

First of all, Ela thought they agreed that Harper wasn't nearly as pretty as she thought she was, and second, since when did being pretty trump academic skills for Kavi Bhatt of all people?

"Look, being smart is the one thing I have," said Kavi.

"I'm not pretty or popular or athletic—" Ela tried to protest, but Kavi cut her off. "It's true. But that's OK because I'm really smart. It's why I matter. It's my thing. It's Gabi and Grace's thing too. And it's just not ... you know."

Not your thing. Ela could almost see the unspoken words hanging between them in a string of LEDs, taunting her.

"So, what is my thing?" said Ela.

Kavi shook her head at Ela like she'd done so many times since explaining that houses weren't supposed to be round. "I don't know. You'll have to figure that out for yourself."

And that, of course, is why Ela is here in this Snowy land, hiding from sketchy dogs in a freezing yurt, telling stories she didn't mean to tell.

25

Ela

SLED-IN-THE-BOX

The only sound in the yurt is of Ela blushing. OK, Ela's blushing doesn't actually make a sound, but if it did, it would be a high-pitched *Why do I always talk too much?* It's like Ela is a balloon, and whenever she's under pressure, her words come out fast and fizzing because otherwise she'll explode. But now she's just told the Princess she's not smart enough to deserve friends.

From the ramp above Ela, the Princess sniffs. "This girl, Kavi, she may be quite bright academically, but has she had even a single hour of etiquette training?"

Ela laughs. "Probably not."

"Well, I have had etiquette training, and I am collecting a lovely assortment of snacks that will make the trip to the castle simply fly by."

"So, about that..." Ela doesn't want to be a pain, but she's not feeling so excited about going to the castle now that she knows it means dealing with Hounds with names like Cunning, who, according to the Princess, might not bite but also might.

"Yes?"

"What do the Hounds look like?" asks Ela. Maybe if she can picture them as actual dogs, they won't seem so scary. After all, she used to be afraid of her neighbours' dog when she was little, and he's the sweetest thing now that she knows him. "Are their ears floppy or maybe their tails? Or their fur?"

"Hmm," says the Princess. "They're rather sleek, I would say. But I wouldn't spend too much time worrying about them. In a kingdom this size, the odds are we won't see them again."

Ela wants to believe her. But if she turned back now, she could keep talking to the Princess all the way to her heated, Hound-free cabin. All in all, it would still be way more than Ela expected for the day. "I just don't know..."

"What is it that you don't know?" asks the Princess. Her footsteps hurry down the spiral ramp that circles the inside of the yurt, getting louder as they pass over Ela's head.

"I don't know how much longer I should stay," admits Ela.

The Princess's steps stop. "Are you suggesting you might leave?"

"Not right this second, but I don't..." Love the idea of possibly vicious Hounds? Or vertigsnow? Or vertigsnow with possibly vicious Hounds?

"Perhaps I could help convince you otherwise?" says the Princess, even though Ela didn't complete her sentence.

Her footsteps start up again until she appears back on the ground floor with her arms filled with all sorts of stuff. "Is there something else in here that could make the journey more comfortable for you? Blankets for warmth, maybe? Mistmir's are very soft. And water-resistant too. Take a look around for whatever you'd like."

Ela is happy to look around inside. It's the outside that's the problem. She steps further into the dark aisle. The boxes toward the back are bigger, each at least two or three feet high and just as wide. Ela tries to lift one perched up high. Instead, she accidentally knocks it down.

Ela walks over to it to pick it up. The box is on its side, with some bolts and a metal tube scattered nearby. It's only when she gets closer that she realizes it's not a tube exactly – it's like a sled runner, but shorter than usual. She puts everything back in the box and starts to push it forward.

"I think I might have found a sled," she says.

"A sled in a box? That's unusual," says the Princess. She moves some of her packages out of the way to make room for Ela in the circle where the sun is shining. "Do you need help?"

"I've got it," says Ela. It's heavy, but she'd like to do it herself, especially if it might be another fail. The box slides slowly, crunching slightly against the grit on the floor. It's made from a funny paper, rougher than cardboard and paler – it reminds her of the time a few years ago at the science museum that she tried to make paper from water and wood pulp, except this box doesn't fall apart after five minutes. Honestly, it's probably years old. The things in this place are such a funny mix of familiar and strange.

"Can you help me put it on its side?" asks Ela once she gets it to the centre of the room. The sun beams down, warming her somewhat.

The Princess does, and Ela kneels, opens the box, and pulls out an armload of pieces. The girls gasp. Ela's seen pieces exactly like this in her dad's lab.

"The sled..." starts Ela. "It belonged to—"

"My father," whispers the Princess. She looks like she's seen a ghost, like Ela's shock has transferred to her.

"You mean *my* father?" says Ela. "This sled belonged to my father."

When Ela was younger, she built a sled just like this with her father once. She was at his lab, and she was sad because he was sad. She can't remember why exactly, except he said, "I'm trying to fix a big mistake, and it's not working."

All Ela wanted to do was make it better, but she didn't know how. "It's OK to make mistakes," she said. "Just keep trying."

"You're right, Eelie-Pie," said her dad. "I'll keep at it. For now, let's get to work."

Building things always made them forget their worries, and the robot sled was a very cool project: instead of having two long runners like a normal sled, it had four telescoping legs, each with a short runner for a foot. When the legs folded up, it functioned pretty much like a normal sled, but when they extended, it could actually walk. The bed was flat, like most sleds, but you could attach solar-panel sides to the flat bed to make an open box to carry things without them falling out. After they put it together and the sled had charged, they decided to play a trick on her mother by hiding Ela in the open compartment of the sled. The sled "walked" to where her mother was working outside.

"Surprise!" Ela popped out.

Her mom yelped, and Ela giggled. But the best part was that her dad was smiling again.

Ela reaches into the box, her fingers fumbling until they find another sled runner. She glances up at the Princess. "I built one just like this with my father. He did most of the work, though."

"So you are familiar with this ... sled?"

"At least one like it." Ela shakes the rest of the pieces out of the box. While some are scraped and scratched, and a few are dented, as far as Ela can tell, nothing big is missing. "If we can reassemble it, we could use it to carry our stuff."

To Ela's surprise, the Princess walks over and starts putting pieces of the sled back into the box. "It would be an excellent plan but for one thing: we absolutely cannot put it back together."

26

The Princess

CUDDLE-LUMP

First of all, it belonged to the Princess's father, not Ela's. This very Hound. Or sled. Actually, this particular sled was only ever a sled. Second of all, the last time the Princess saw it, the sled was completely and violently destroyed. She didn't ever expect to see it again, and now here it is, in pieces, with Ela of all people trying to put it together.

"What are you even talking about?" says Ela. She reaches into the box and starts to take out all the parts the Princess just put away.

"There's no point in rebuilding it. That sled is not functional anymore."

Ela crinkles her nose. "I don't know. It looks like it could be. Some of the pieces are already connected."

"Yes, but the whole thing was damaged. It won't work."

"But my dad told me these sleds are modular. So even if

it was taken apart, it can be put back together pretty easily. It can't hurt to try."

"I don't … I didn't realize that … I suppose if you want to…" murmurs the Princess. First Ela and now the sled. This day will be the end of her. The Princess needs some space. She busies herself in the gardening section, away from Ela laying out the sled pieces.

"I think pretty much everything is here," Ela says. "There's only one problem. There aren't any instructions."

The Princess's chest tightens. That's just what she said to her father when they first opened the box.

They'd both been told to meet in the Green Room in the family quarters of the castle at precisely 4.00 that afternoon. The Princess was not yet ten years old, and she walked nervously to the meeting spot, unsure of whether her father would show up. But he was there, along with a large box from the Beyond Lands tied with a bow in the Mistmir style.

"Shall we open it together?" she asked.

He nodded but made no move toward the box.

"I'll do the bow," she said.

He nodded again, glancing at the clock. He pulled his cloak around him, though the Princess thought the room was warm enough. Usually, royalty only chose to wear a royal cloak for formal events, though lately the King was wearing it more and more around the castle, even during the day when he had nowhere else to be.

"We can just take a quick look today, sir. I'm sure you're very busy."

"As the King, my schedule is my own," he replied, but he still kept his distance, as if he wasn't sure if the giver meant to give a gift or play a trick on him.

The Princess began taking the pieces out. Most were heavier than expected, and all were strange. Even the screws and bolts were a funny, overly silver colour. She was going to comment on that, when the King came over and sat beside her. Wordlessly, he began rearranging pieces here and there. When the box was emptied, the Princess knew exactly what it was, for the King had put all of the pieces in the approximate shape of the carrying sleds for which the Strangers were famous.

"There's a problem. There aren't any instructions," the Princess said.

"Even better," said the King. For the first time all afternoon, the Princess thought she caught the hint of a smile.

The following day, they met again in the same room at precisely 4 p.m. Before they got to work, the King placed his royal cloak neatly over a chair. Then he showed her how to hold a screw-turner to get the maximum torque and how the wires were colour coded to make clear which went where. He began to assemble one of the legs, and the

Princess tried to follow his moves with another, though it wasn't easy to keep up.

She worked up her nerve to ask, "Sir, why were you happy there were no instructions?"

"Instructions would have made it too easy. Don't you agree?"

The Princess paused. She wasn't sure she did.

"You don't have to. You might be more like your mother in this regard, more talented with words than mechanics. Everyone tells the story about how we met when I went to a library, and she helped me with various books and such. It's not false, but did you know I helped her too? She was trying to translate an instruction manual from another language and couldn't find the words, but from the diagrams, I helped her. That part is never talked about. Now, to be sure, she was brilliant in ways no one else in the Kingdom was."

The Princess said nothing, afraid that if she spoke, he would change the subject.

"I know they say I'm not very smart, but I married her despite all the talk about a Trader's daughter being a more suitable match. If that doesn't prove I'm wise..."

"You certainly are, sir," said the Princess.

He smiled at her. For the rest of the hour, they worked together in silence.

The following day, they met again at the same time in the same room. They checked that each of the legs extended and retracted properly and then snapped a foot-runner on each one. They experimented with various fasteners to see which went where. They tested the bed of the sled to ensure it could hold a person's weight. Not more than twenty words were spoken, but by the time they finished, all four legs were attached to the bed of the sled. The Princess wasn't sure she'd ever had a better afternoon.

The fourth day they met, they focused on the finer details, connecting wires and the smallest pieces.

As they settled on the carpet to work, the King spoke. "Did you know this used to be my playroom when I was young? Perhaps 'playroom' isn't the right word. Maybe workshop."

"Why don't you have a workshop now, sir?"

"Can you imagine what my advisers would say? I'm supposed to be king. Besides, there's nothing special about being able to tinker. Being royalty, on the other hand ... that's the definition of special, isn't it?"

Was it? She was enjoying tinkering with her father far more than she ever enjoyed doing her royal duties.

She took her time with her work, not wanting to make a mistake, not wanting the project to be over. But she was almost finished before the hour was up.

"Did you ever want a pet?" asked the Princess as they began to test the sensors on the memory box.

"I did want a dog when I was young," said the King. "But of course, we weren't allowed to have pets in the living area of the castle. You know the rule, Karina: You can go to the stables if you'd like to play with animals."

"Yes, sir. What I meant to say was perhaps we could pretend with the sled."

The King tilted the memory box "head" so it was looking up at him and chuckled. The Princess wasn't sure she had ever made him laugh before.

"We'll have to think of a name," he said. "Other than that, though, I think we've about completed this project."

"Perhaps we could do another, sir. If you have the time."

"Which he doesn't." Lord Hesketh was leaning in the doorway.

The Princess's stomach turned to ice. How long had he been standing there, spying on her special time with her father?

"Is this where you've been hiding out, sir? We've missed your royal acumen. There are a number of proposals that require your input – defensive strategies and the like," said Lord Hesketh.

They were in a private section of the castle, with no one but family and designated servants allowed. And her father had spent only an hour each day with her. Lord Hesketh could discuss his proposals with him any other time. Looking back, the Princess wonders if it would have made any difference if she had said one of those things instead of what she did say: "The Mists are all the defence the Kingdom needs."

“Is that so? Did that toy you’ve got there come from within Mistmir or from those that breached its boundaries?” Lord Hesketh turned to the King before she could respond. “Sir, we do have some urgent matters to discuss. We’re relying on your superior judgement to proceed.”

The King stood up straight and nodded solemnly as he fastened his royal cloak. The Princess had to fight an urge to hold on to it and ask him to stay. But though she remained still, he turned to her, and for an instant his bearing softened.

“I suppose,” said the King as he gave the Princess a sad smile. “I suppose that is where I’m needed most. Enjoy the toy, Karina.”

It’s not a toy, she almost said. Instead, she remained silent, trying to come up with the perfect response that would keep her father with her and make Lord Hesketh disappear. But for all her supposed talent with words, she never did figure out what that would be.

Now, as she watches Ela working diligently, she realizes that the sled could be the key to convincing Ela to stay in the Kingdom. Whatever memories the Princess has of this sled need to be forgotten. She needs to focus on one goal, and that is getting Ela to the castle. The Princess forces herself to take her sack, spade and blankets and sit by Ela.

“It looks like you’re making excellent progress,” says the Princess.

Ela holds up a metal tube at various angles, then snaps it into place. "It's actually in better shape than I thought."

"I'm glad to hear it. May I help?"

Ela shoots her a strange look, which is understandable given the Princess's initial reaction.

"Could you help me with the solar panel?" says Ela, lifting a glassy, dark rectangle.

Without a word, the Princess grabs the other side, and together they place it where it connects with the bed of the sled. The Princess makes some small adjustments to line it up perfectly, and when she finishes, Ela is next to her with the screw-turner to attach it. They do the same for the other three sides. They don't talk much, and they work quickly. It's surprising how much it reminds the Princess of working with the King, considering there couldn't be two people more different.

"We just need to attach the memory box and the handle," says the Princess.

"Memory box?" asks Ela.

"That's where it stores the instructions, so it knows what to do. You can train them to do all sorts of things, to recognize—" The Princess cuts herself off.

"Oh, you mean a computer?" says Ela. "All the sleds have them, and they're networked. So if you program one, the newer sleds can learn from the older. Though it's not exactly learning, since they're not alive." She squints as the

Princess attaches the memory box where a head would go. "It kind of looks like it could be, though."

"I beg your pardon?"

"Doesn't it look kind of like an animal? I think we should give it a face and a tail."

Ela is smiling innocently. The Princess swallows hard. She doesn't want to make a big deal of what was clearly meant as a harmless request. And perhaps, since the sled has a body and retractable legs, and a head-like memory box with two eye-like light sensors, it's not entirely surprising Ela would come to that conclusion.

"What would you propose to use?" asks the Princess.

"If you don't mind using some snacks, I think one of those doughnut-cookie things would make a really good nose."

"I beg your pardon?" says the Princess as Ela unpacks a sweetberry dough cookie and sticks it on a screw protruding from the memory box.

"It's a nose." Ela nods. "Let's give it ears and a tail!"

The Princess can feel herself sweating under her coat. "I'll go look for something," she says, forcing cheer into her voice. She rushes to the miscellaneous section and hides while Ela rips some sort of wrapper. A tail! Really? The Princess glances around for the most un-Hound-like tail she can find. Fork, no ... belt, no ... screw-turner, no ... feather duster ... yes.

"It's perfect!" exclaims Ela as the Princess walks over,

wood-finch-feather duster in hand. "Do you like the ears?" Ela has folded squares of dried fruit in quarters, making neat triangular ears.

"Indeed, I do," says the Princess. This has got to stop before Ela gets any more ideas.

"What kind of animal do you think it is?" says Ela, stepping back and squinting.

"Snort-hog," says the Princess. She's not going to give Ela time to come up with any other options.

Ela squints. "It does look kind of like a pig, with that round nose. We made a sled-pig! Should we give it a name?"

"Cuddle-Lump," says the Princess. She's not even sure where that came from, except that it's the least Hound-like name she could think of.

"Cuddle-Lump? But it's not at all ... Oh, I get it!" Ela looks curiously at the Princess. "I didn't know you could be funny." She claps her hand to her mouth as soon as the words are out. It's rather endearing, actually.

"Yes, I've learned to hide it well," says the Princess. "Shall we?" She packs a sack full of snacks and couple of blankets in the sled's open compartment. Then she takes the spade with one hand and, with the other, motions to the door and grabs Cuddle-Lump by its leash-like handle. "I think it's time to show Cuddle-Lump Mistmir."

27

The Princess

DON'T FORGET ME

There are three ways down into the valley, and all of them are bad. The first is the Meander Path, which is at the far side of the Royal Ridge. It is slow and winding and thick with trees. Perhaps more to the point, Ela has been on it before, and who knows if she'd remember if she saw it again. It's out of the question. The second way down is the Royal Slope, which starts at the summit of the Royal Ridge and shoots straight down to the river across from a side entrance to the castle. It is the fastest way, but it's open, so they could be spotted easily, and the Princess isn't sure how well Ela would do on an incline that steep. Or, rather, she is: Ela would not do well at all. The last way is the Downhill Path, which flanks the other side of the Royal Slope. The most the Princess can say for it is that it's not the other two.

The Princess easily guides Cuddle-Lump, packed with snacks and blankets, to the Downhill Path. Ela said she didn't need the blankets, but the Princess caught her shivering in the yurt. There are rumours of Strangers in centuries past being found frozen to death on the edge of the Mists. The Princess doesn't know if they are true, but she does know that for all their inventions, the Beyond Lands lack certain basic protections against the cold – no special tea to ward off the cold for hours, no yak-oose fur coats, no feather-lined, flint-treaded boots. The Princess feels a stab of regret for not giving Ela Warming Tea at the cottage when she had the chance.

"Is this the quickest way to your house?" asks Ela.

"The Downhill Path is the best way to get there, yes," says the Princess.

"Can you climb up the Downhill Path?"

"Of course. Why wouldn't you?"

"Uh, because it's called the Downhill Path," says Ela, emphasizing the *down*. "Is there an Uphill Path?"

"No, though I suppose there ought to be," says the Princess. "Perhaps we should change the name of the Meander Path, which is the one people usually take up because it's less steep."

"Less steep sounds good. Could we rename the Meander Path '*Ela's* Downhill Path'?" Ela grins and puts her arms out for balance as they start to descend.

The girl is funny, but also, no, absolutely not.

Ela's smile suddenly disappears. "Did you hear that?"

"Hear what?" As soon as the words leave the Princess's mouth, the rhythmic clomping hits her ears. "A Hound!"

"I don't think so," says Ela. "It sounded more like a machine or something?"

The Princess swallows, trying to push down the feeling of her heart in her throat.

"You need to hide." The Princess scans the familiar landscape. Unsurprisingly, all she sees are Snow and trees, which, unless you are a very tiny child, do not make good hiding places. And even then, not so much.

"But you said we wouldn't—" says Ela.

"Shh! Hide or at least stand back and stay very still." The Princess grabs the spade from the sled and strides forward, hoping to put some distance between where the Hound might stop and Ela. Though she's gripping the handle hard, she forces her face to be neutral. She's been told the Hounds technically only "hear" and "see", but the Princess always worries that on some deeper level they've been trained to sense fear.

Within a minute, the Hound appears from the trees. It's not Cunning. It's Biter, so named for the teeth stuck to its jaws, teeth that previously belonged to other predators. As always when she sees it, the Princess has to fight the urge to run, which is silly, because it could outrun her or any human.

It stops three arm's-lengths away. The Princess stays

very still as it moves its head up and down, evaluating her. She wishes she could toss it a snack from the yurt to distract it, but perhaps this is one more reason the King prefers these Hounds to the normal kind – they do not get distracted.

Biter stretches its jaw. For a moment, the Princess stops breathing, but then she remembers: this is Biter. It shows its fangs every time. It extends its legs, ready to circle her.

Clomp. Clomp. Clomp.

Every Hound's march sounds the same. Like a soldier on inspection duty.

But the more the Princess thinks about it, the more she welcomes the scrutiny. A Hound focused on her is a Hound not focused on Ela.

It faces her again. The Princess stares into its orbs, glowing red now. She wonders if there's something more she should do to keep it fixed on her. She could shake the spade at it. Or even poke it. Well, poking it might be too much. But a shake? Maybe?

Before she can decide, Biter's head bows slightly, as it does every time it decides its find is not a threat. It collapses on its sled-runner feet. The Princess exhales as it slides backward.

And then it turns, straight towards Cuddle-Lump and Ela.

"No!"

Biter doesn't even slow down.

She chases it, spade in hand, while quickly scanning the landscape for a stick. She's seen Biter play fetch with the King. It's a long shot, but worth a try? But the Princess can't find one. And, as she reaches Cuddle-Lump, she can't find Ela either.

The girl is gone.

The Princess approaches Biter from behind while it approaches Cuddle-Lump. The sled-pig should be all too familiar. But with a cookie nose? And a feather duster tail? And pressed-fruit ears? And a big blanket-covered lump in the open compartment? Why did she ever agree to let Ela dress up Cuddle-Lump?

Wait. A blanket-covered lump? Oh!

The Princess has found Ela. Her hiding place is much better and much, much worse than a tree could ever be. The Princess grips the spade as Biter opens its jaw again. Could she knock out its teeth? Or would it be better to try for a swift blow to the head? Or would that alert all the other Hounds to come? Biter at least is oblivious to her swirl of thoughts. It's wholly focused on the sled that holds Ela, curled up.

Biter tilts its head, considering. The Princess tightens her grip on the spade.

Biter slides another arm's-length forward.

Stop. Sense.

Stand. Sense.

Circle. Sense.

Stop again. Sense.

Cuddle-Lump and the Ela lump stay still, but the Princess raises the spade so it is knee-high. Not enough to tip Biter off, she hopes.

Go, go, go, thinks the Princess. *Please, just go.*

Biter rests on its foot-runners. It glides away.

The Princess slumps against an ice-oak with relief.

"Don't forget me!"

The Princess jumps at the voice and drops the spade. Before she can pick it up again, Biter is back. The Hound starts barking. The Princess lifts the spade from the Snow. This time she doesn't bother being subtle about her intentions.

"Don't forget me!" Ela's voice is muffled and weird but loud. Shockingly loud. "Don't forget me!"

Bark. Bark. Bark. Bark.

"Don't forget me!"

Bark. Bark. Bark. Bark. Clomp. Clomp. Clomp. Clomp. Biter marches around the sled at inspection pace.

The Ela-shaped lump quivers a bit. But it doesn't stop calling out. If the Princess weren't paralysed with some combination of fear and rage, she would march over, grab that blanket off Ela, and tell her to shut up.

"Don't forget me! Don't forget me!"

Bark. Bark. Bark. Bark! Bark. Bark. Bark. Bark!

Biter's circles are getting tighter and tighter around Ela, who is noticeably shaking. But at least, finally, it appears that she has decided to stop yelling.

Biter stops barking. It backs up.

The sound of the Princess's own breathing fills her ears. The spade is shaking in her hands. As the worst of her fear passes, she realizes she is truly, deeply annoyed.

And maybe Biter is too. It chomps its jaw and, after a few more head tilts, slides away fast, down the Downhill Path.

"What in the King's name was that about?" says the Princess, yanking the blanket off Ela. "What's the point of hiding if you can't keep quiet?"

"Why are you yelling at me?" says Ela, climbing out of the sled-pig. "I hid like you told me. I didn't even get up when you kept shouting, 'Don't forget me.'"

"Me? That was you!"

"No, it wasn't. It was your accent," says Ela.

The Princess does not have an accent! "I didn't say a word the whole time."

"I didn't either," says Ela, hands on her hips.

"Well, it wasn't a wood-finch. And it certainly wasn't me. So who was it?" She grabs Cuddle-Lump's handle and gives it a satisfying tug.

There's a creak and a squeak as the sled-pig rises to a standing position.

"At your service," says Cuddle-Lump.

The Princess drops the handle in shock. With a quick whirr, the sled-pig promptly slides backward off the Downhill Path.

28

The Princess

(NO) SCHOOL AND (NO) FRIENDS

The Princess runs down the embankment after Cuddle-Lump. It's speeding up, away from her, and before she can reach it, it crashes into an ice-oak. As the contents of the sled fly into the air, the Princess could swear she heard a long burp and more words.

"What in the King's name was that?" she mutters to herself, jogging toward the mess.

"A gift, especially for you!" replies Cuddle-Lump.

And that's when the Princess realizes. It's not Ela's voice. Or the Princess's. It's the silly, jokey voice of Auntie Nithya – Ela's mother – captured long before Ela was born. They need to get to the castle as soon as possible, before Ela recognizes it. And with silly old Cuddle-Lump piping up randomly, that could be any second.

"I think I figured out why it started talking," says Ela, edging her way down the embankment. "It's the solar panels. They charged the batteries and turned the sled on."

Ela is probably right. The Princess never took Cuddle-Lump outside. But if it's charged now, that's all the more reason to not take it with them. Who knows what else it might say or do?

"That's an interesting theory. It does seem to be behaving quite erratically, perhaps because of its previous damage," says the Princess. "What would you think about leaving it behind? It may be slowing us down."

"Are you serious? Cuddle-Lump just saved me from the Hound."

The Princess can't deny that. Well, if they have to keep the sled, they may as well have some snacks. "Have you ever had chocolate before? It's wonderful stuff, if you'd like to try it."

Ela gives her a strange look. "Yes, I've had chocolate. I like it a lot."

The Princess hands her a piece. "Let's backtrack to the Royal Ridge and then descend the Royal Slope. It's by far the fastest way to the castle." And the easiest for spotting Hounds.

Ela bites her lip. "The Royal Slope? Is it steep?"

"I'll help you. I've probably made the descent a thousand times. And in the meantime, perhaps we could get back to the storytelling. You could share something about your family? Or another story about school or friends?" Isn't that what normal children with normal childhoods talk about?

Ela swallows her chocolate and shakes her head. "You're the one who is supposed to be telling stories. You could tell me about *your* school and *your* friends? Or maybe about the Hounds? Something was really weird about the one that came. I didn't see it, but it just didn't sound right at all."

"School and friends it is!" says the Princess.

The only issue with this otherwise harmless topic is that the Princess never went to school, and she has no friends. As far as she can tell, most royalty doesn't. Sometimes royalty has siblings, who might be your friend or, according to Madame Vidya's history books, might lock you in a tower so they can have a clean shot at the throne.

But a real friend – someone you just hang out with and do silly projects with and not even notice the time passing? Something like what she and Ela might be starting to have? But no. If she and Ela were really friends, she would tell her the whole story, not just the convenient parts. And she wouldn't be taking her to the castle to trap her, even for a little while. The Princess is quite sure friends don't do that.

"So, as far as school goes, I didn't attend a normal school," says the Princess.

"You were homeschooled?" asks Ela.

Homeschooled. Schooled at home? The Princess never thought about it that way. "I was taught in the same building where I lived, so yes, I suppose you would call that homeschooling? But I had a tutor."

"Is homeschooling common here?"

The Princess studies Ela for a second. Has Auntie Nithya mentioned she was homeschooled too? "Not particularly. As a princess, I had to learn all the academic subjects but also things like etiquette and leadership. The thought was that having a one-on-one tutor like Madame Vidya would permit me to progress more quickly."

"I suppose you knew all your multiplication tables by the time you were eight, and you were superfast," says Ela.

"Seven, actually, and yes, I was quite fast, not that it mattered."

"At my school it would totally matter. You would have been in the advanced maths class for sure."

"And had the joy of learning with classmates who thought their mathematics placement was more important than basic courtesy." The Princess shakes her head. "It's preposterous that your school had a race about that."

"I guess that's an advantage of being homeschooled. No maths races," says Ela.

"Though I always thought one advantage to a regular school would be that you're less likely to be lonely. Not that I was, exactly. Sometimes I would play along with the other children from my window. Rope-jump was my favourite. You know, where the kids chant their silly rhymes, and you see how many times you can jump over a rope without missing."

The Princess starts chanting:

Something from this land, something from that.

A silk-wool rug, a water jug, a yak-oose fur hat.

Could be something common, could be something rare,

But if you've got nothing, then you're going nowhere!

How many items do you have? One, two, three, four . . .

The Princess catches herself before she gets to five. Giving secrets away about how to leave Mistmir! She is entirely too comfortable with this girl.

The Princess speeds up, yanking Cuddle-Lump forward. "At your service!" it pipes up, sliding backward. The Princess gives the handle a gentler tug, and it starts moving in the right direction again.

"So anyway, I made it to a hundred and eighty-seven on my left foot and two hundred and sixty on my right. That was higher than I saw any other kids do, though of course I didn't brag to any of the children, because that wouldn't be polite. But my nanny, aunt, and tutor were all quite impressed. Perhaps my schooling was different from most other kids', but what else would you expect for a princess?"

29

The Princess

WINNING THE BATTLE BUT LOSING THE WAR

The truth is, the Princess would have loved to have gone to a real school. After she broke the rope-jump record, she launched a campaign for that very purpose. She didn't target her father, for she knew he didn't appreciate it when she made a fuss. But every day for weeks, she'd badger Amma, Auntie Nithya, and most of all Madame Vidya. "Why can't I go to school? Everyone *else* gets to go." When whining didn't work, she tried logic: "I can do extra homework in the evenings. I'll build better connections with our citizens. I'll understand our Kingdom better."

Amma laughed her off. "My grandkids beg me to let them stay home from school, and you beg me to let you go. Isn't that the way of it?"

Auntie Nithya just shrugged. "Kiri, this is what works for now. You'll have the freedom to learn in different ways when you're older."

Madame Vidya simply said nothing. Until the day she couldn't take it anymore and exclaimed, "Really, child, you'll have me out of a job!"

A job? A job! Was that all the Princess was to her? The Princess understood that many people in the castle had jobs: the cooks who cooked, the guards who guarded, the maids who cleaned, the gardeners who gardened, the stable masters who kept up the stables. But Madame Vidya, with whom she spent more waking hours than anyone else? Who taught her right and wrong, and praised and corrected her but always, always seemed to care for her? She only did this because she was paid? And Amma too?

The only thing more embarrassing than this realization was the fact that the Princess hadn't understood it all along. For seven solid days, the Princess refused to answer Madame Vidya's vocabulary questions even though they both knew the Princess knew them cold. For seven solid nights, the Princess refused to let Amma put her hair into her nighttime braids, even though that meant it was extra tangled in the morning. When they asked her what was wrong, the Princess had to bite her tongue to keep from saying, *Isn't it your* job *to know?*

By the following week, being contrary grew tiring, but the Princess had learned her lesson. She needed to focus on the people who loved her best even if it wasn't their job. Family. With her father always preoccupied with his royal duties, that meant Auntie Nithya. The Princess wanted to be the person who greeted her at breakfast and relaxed with her at dinner. She wanted to follow her aunt on her trips to the farming villages, her tours of the Yurts of Plenty, her visits to the harbour to welcome returning ships. She would wait outside royal council meetings so she could see her aunt as soon as they'd adjourn. The Princess had her classes and duties, but the rest of her time was reserved for Auntie Nithya.

But all of Auntie Nithya's time was not reserved for the Princess. Some days, when Madame Vidya rewarded the Princess with an extra break for her hard work, Auntie Nithya was nowhere to be found: not by the river, not in the library, not with the King. Some nights, after Auntie Nithya had kissed the Princess good night, her footsteps would patter down the stairs, and when the Princess looked out her window, she would see her aunt's shadowy figure disappear in the moonlight. When the Princess finally worked up the nerve to ask where she was going, Auntie Nithya flushed and smiled to herself. "Nowhere," she said.

That was impossible. Everywhere was somewhere.

The Princess didn't want to meddle. She understood that proper etiquette meant you did not snoop. But she also knew that Auntie Nithya was keeping something important from her, and curiosity was flooding her like a storm-swollen river.

One afternoon, when the King was locked in his study

with Lord Hesketh, Amma was watching her grandkids, and Madame Vidya had left early with a particularly bad cold, the Princess caught the familiar creak of footsteps on the side turret stairs. Sure enough, within a minute, Auntie Nithya came into view, skiing toward the Meander Path.

The Princess threw on her coat, pulled her hood over her head, and wrapped a scarf around the bottom half of her face. She strapped on her uphill skis and, keeping a safe distance, followed her aunt.

The best part of the Meander Path, with its twists and turns and tall, thick trees, was how easily you could track someone without being noticed. All the Princess had to do was let Auntie Nithya's long, elegant ski tracks guide her. But as they turned toward the Highlands Glade, the Princess got a strange feeling in her stomach. She was heading toward the Strangers' Settlement.

To be clear, the Princess liked the Strangers. Not because of the flutterbyes they gave her each birthday or the other contraptions they had brought to Mistmir, but because they exuded intelligence and purpose. They mostly kept to themselves, but when they were invited to join the Kingdom's festivities, they would. Sometimes they would bring small items, like sun squares or microscopes, and show the children how they worked. Though the Princess kept a polite distance, she found the demonstrations just as fascinating as the other children did. The Strangers seemed to treat everyone with respect and no one with fear, and the Princess thought that was how she would like to act when she became Queen. But as much as she liked the Strangers, this would be her first time in their settlement.

Before she could get there, she stumbled upon Auntie Nithya and the Stranger named Neel in the woods. The Princess froze and, quiet as a snow rabbit, backed up behind a blue-birch tree. But the couple probably wouldn't have noticed if she'd stomped around like a yak-cow or grunted like a snort-hog. They were kissing like they breathed each other, not air.

The person the Princess loved most in this world had someone she loved even more.

Without the couple noticing, the Princess rushed back to the castle, waited until the King finished his meetings for the day, then marched into his office and told him what she had seen. For once, he didn't seem distracted. He listened to her intently. The next morning, he even invited her to join him on the announcement balcony while he made a royal proclamation. For the first time, she stood to his right in Auntie Nithya's spot while Lord Hesketh stood to his left. There, the King issued the official decree ordering the Strangers to leave as soon as the rivers thawed.

This was an example of what Madame Vidya called "winning the battle but losing the war". Because when the Strangers left – and this time, they'd be gone for years – Auntie Nithya left with them.

30

The Princess

AUNTIE NITHYA'S LETTER

The Princess found the letter on her desk the evening after the Strangers' departure:

Dearest Karina,

There's so much I wanted to tell you before leaving, but maybe it is better to write it all down. Sometimes the most important thoughts and biggest feelings can get garbled when I try to speak them, and I want to be completely clear.

First, I sense that you may blame yourself for my departure. Please don't. I had already been planning to leave with Neel this spring. In fact, I had been trying to find the right time to tell you. While the circumstances of my leaving were a bit more dramatic than anticipated, the actual outcome was not.

It's no secret that though I was born a royal, I wasn't born for royalty. You've heard the rumours that I wanted to be a Trader. They're not entirely false. While I didn't have any interest in trading, I wanted to go beyond the Mists as soon as I knew it was a possibility. I thought I would try after I completed my studies and training.

But life is not predictable, and a series of tragedies and joys kept me here: the tragedy of losing my father, your grandfather, the previous King; the joy of my brother's wedding to your lovely mother; the tragedy of her untimely death; and the joy of having you.

I've stayed for over a decade longer than I expected. I could have left earlier; you would have been in excellent hands with Amma and Madame Vidya. There aren't two people in this Kingdom with more love and knowledge. But I wanted to help raise you, to learn who you were as a person, to see who you would become. I had to leave this year, but I do so fully knowing your strength, your goodness, and your dedication. You have more of those than any of the King's advisers ever did, myself included. You will be excellent at whatever you choose to do, and if you ultimately choose to rule Mistmir, you will be the ruler our beautiful land deserves.

It was preposterous for Aunt Nithya to suggest any other option, but the Princess appreciated the compliment nonetheless.

As for your father: my hope is that in my absence he will no longer feel like he has to pick sides between his bickering advisers. I also hope he will allow himself to enjoy being a parent. You make him so very proud. Now that I'm leaving, I think it would be wonderful for you two to spend more time together. In fact, Neel and I have left a project for both of you that I hope you will enjoy. It is in the Green Room in the family quarters, which was your father's favourite place to play and build in as a child. Meet him there next Monday at 4 p.m. Open the box together and have fun with it!

Finally, I will be back. I don't know exactly when, but someday when the rivers are flowing and we find space in the Mists, I'll return. The first thing I'll want to do is to see you.

All my love,

Auntie Nithya

P.S. I've left you a few surprise messages in the gift. I hope they will make you smile!

31

Ela

THE CAULDRON OF LONELINESS

"Don't forget me!" says Cuddle-Lump as the girls reach the Royal Ridge. The weirdest thing is that every time Ela hears those staticky pre-recorded words, she is certain she is forgetting something. She's just not sure what.

When she crests the summit and sees a grey castle in the distance, lording over a town with a river winding through it, a memory comes back. The castle with red, green, gold and blue flags waving from the top. No purple, her favourite colour. A busy town with all sorts of people, including her parents and her neighbours, Ms Ambika and Ms V.

Or maybe she doesn't remember any of this; maybe this is just her imagination on overdrive after this strange, strange day. Purple still is her favourite colour. Either way, from up on the ridge, there are no signs of life in the valley, no bustling in the buildings. It's like she's standing on the rim of a cauldron of loneliness.

Her biggest issue now, though, is not loneliness, but the cliff at her feet.

"Aren't you coming?" says the Princess.

Ela bites her lip. "Could we maybe go the other way down?" She points to the winding, gentler path. "I know you said it's slower, but I just don't think I can hike down this without falling on my face. Or my butt."

Oops. Probably shouldn't say the word "butt" to a Princess. But she doesn't seem to be bothered. Instead, she nods thoughtfully.

"Perhaps there is another solution." The Princess looks down at Cuddle-Lump with a smile. She takes out the spade, blankets and food sack.

Ela follows her gaze to the sled-pig's empty compartment. The Princess can't mean for her to— "No! That is not a good idea."

"It's brilliant. We know you fit, albeit tightly. You sit, I'll pull you, we'll be down in no time."

"*You'll* pull me down the mountain?"

"I think it's better if I control Cuddle-Lump. It's proving to be somewhat unpredictable. But – and I do not mean to brag – I'm quite agile in the Snow, and I've hiked down this slope with tools and sacks of food many, many times. Guiding a sled should be no problem at all."

"I don't know," says Ela. Actually, she does know. This is a terrible idea.

"I think we both are hoping to move quickly. And I can't think of any way faster." The Princess rummages through the cloth sack and unwraps a small package of golden leathery fruit. "Can I offer you a snack for the ride? Dried sunapples. Mistmir's finest."

Sunapples?

Sunapples???

Sunapples do not exist.

On her first day of kindergarten, Ela drew a picture of a giant sunapple. Kavi, sitting at the desk next to her, drawing a perfect strawberry, informed Ela: "There's no such thing as sunapples." Ela asked her teacher, Ms Chan, who said maybe she was thinking of plain old apples or peaches or apricots, but definitely not sunapples, because, like Kavi had said, there was no such fruit. Before that, Ela had asked her parents not just for sunapples, but sunapple cake and sunapple pie and even sunapple ice cream, and they always said, "That's not something we can get you." But Ela thought they just meant the grocery store was out. She hadn't realized sunapples didn't exist until Kavi and her teacher said so.

"Did you say 'sunapples'?"

"Yes. Honestly, in my opinion, they're as delicious as chocolate, and I'm not just saying that because they're the official fruit of Mistmir." The Princess offers Ela a shiny yellow fruit strip.

Ela takes it from her and sniffs the melon-vanilla scent. Joy stirs in her chest. She is suddenly, inexplicably happy. She stuffs it in her mouth and shuts her eyes. Her senses explode: she's filled with the scent of spiced sunapple cider and flaky sunapple pastries, the sound of horse-drawn carts and chattering families, the feel of cold air on her face when the rest of her is cozy warm, a taste of pear and peach, melon and vanilla, and a hint of apples. A scene is coming to her: castle walls and gargoyles. Icicles hang off the gargoyles' stone snouts as if they have runny noses. The stained glass of the castle windows spray colour on the snowy grounds. A golden spot shines like a sunapple, but, disappointingly, it is just light.

She opens her eyes back up. The scene is gone except for the grey castle in the valley. If she's going to find answers in this kingdom, that's where they'll be. The Princess is right. She needs to get there as soon as possible.

"OK," she says, nodding to the Princess.

"Just climb in and I'll turn it around."

Ela takes a deep breath and then smooshes herself into the sled, curling her body in the tightest ball possible. The Princess tugs sharply at the sled, then lets go to adjust her grip.

"At your service!" exclaims Cuddle-Lump.

And before the Princess can grab its handle or Ela can scream, it goes flying backward, straight down the Royal Slope.

32

Ela

REVENGE OF THE BLACK DIAMONDS

Ela does not like downhill skiing. The few times she went with her parents, she only attempted the bunny slopes, and even that felt like a lot. But in this moment, it's like revenge of the black diamonds, as if the steepest slope on every mountain she's avoided has now caught up with her. She is flying down the sharpest incline she can imagine. Backward. In a sled shaking so hard, it could fall apart at any second.

Clangs and shudders fill her ears, along with the steady screech of Snow. She forces herself to open one eye, but she's in a cloud of silver. She can't see a thing. She clutches the sides of the sled tighter. Weirdly, the image of her dad talking about vibrating water molecules comes into her head. Only she's the molecule now.

Ela didn't think the sled could move any faster, but she swears it's picking up speed. Her mittens are terrible for gripping, and the shaking is making it nearly impossible to hang on. She can't help but wonder how far she is from the bottom of the slope. She can't last much longer. She tries to imagine the hill evening out.

Cuddle-Lump lurches hard. Ela flies. The cloud of silver dissipates, and the ground, glaringly bright, rushes to meet her.

Thud.

She's in the Snow.

She can't even remember what number fail this is for the day.

The good thing about a land of Snow is that all your falls are cushioned. The bad thing is that Snow has this metallic taste and smell and tries to fill in any gaps, so if you land face first, it's like eating a mouthful of foil while also getting it up your nose. Ela sits up as quickly as she can and wipes off her face.

She looks up the mountain. The Princess is running toward her. She can faintly hear the Princess yelling, "Are you all right? Are you all right?" Ela stands and takes a few steps. She actually is OK. The feather duster tail isn't far from her, and she rescues it before the Snow swallows it up. Then she waves it at the Princess to show she's fine.

She turns around. What she sees stuns her almost as much as her accidental descent down the mountain. She's close enough to the castle and the town to get a good look. Scratch whatever she imagined it would be.

Everything has changed.

33

The Princess

THE STATE OF THE CASTLE

"I am so, so sorry." The Princess has been taught to limit her apologies to situations where one is strictly warranted, but in this case, it seems like one is in order. "Are you certain you're all right?"

"Fine," murmurs Ela. She is staring straight ahead at the castle, oblivious to everything else, even Cuddle-Lump, which miraculously landed on its sled-runner feet and, less miraculously, is repeatedly saying, "A gift, especially for you! A gift, especially for you!"

"You're not hurt at all? Or have your snow dizziness?" asks the Princess.

"I'm OK," says Ela.

She doesn't look OK, though. She squints her eyes and crinkles her nose. Her mouth hangs slightly open, and she doesn't bother covering it. Then it hits the Princess: Ela isn't reacting to her fall but to the castle itself. She doesn't want to get angry at Ela, but this is the most elegant building in

Mistmir. It's fit for a king, and if it's not good enough for Ela, she can just go home.

(Figuratively speaking, that is. Literally speaking, she has to go with the Princess, of course.)

The Princess clears her throat, ready to point out every fine detail that Ela is missing, every feature Ela would remember if she'd been older when she left.

But when the Princess eyes the castle, the wind is knocked out of her. She sees what Ela must. An empty town, as barren as the highlands they just left behind. No people, no animals, no clamour. Not even whispers. No flags fly from the spires because the spires are gone. Over time, they were no match for the ice. The stained glass is clouded, the castle stones as dull as wash water. Patches of slow-growing snow-moss and ice-lichens have mottled the walls. Even the bridges that cross the Meander River seem to be sagging – under the weight of Snow or maybe just time.

The King told her time would stand still. But as the Princess takes in the deterioration, she knows: it didn't even slow down.

"Are you OK? Princess?"

The Princess blinks. Ela is talking to her. In her shock, it's as if the Princess has forgotten everything Madame Vidya taught her. That won't do at all, especially not now that they're so close. While the Princess truly did intend to pull Ela down safely, it is also true that they've made it a good nine-tenths of the way to the castle in the fastest way possible.

"It's kind of you to ask. Shall we check on Cuddle-Lump and keep moving?" She reaches into the snack sack and pulls out a sweetberry dough cookie. "I believe we'll need to replace its nose and ears, but other than that, it appears to be in good shape." She racks her brain for a suitable question. "Do you have any pets where you live?"

"Pets?" Even though the bottom part of the Royal Slope isn't nearly as steep as the top, Ela takes each step carefully. "Nope. My dad says he's allergic to dogs, though I think he just might be scared of them. But we don't even have fish or hamsters. What about you? Other than those Hounds."

The Hounds! The Princess looks over each of her shoulders. She exhales. Just Snow. For now, at least.

"No pets of my own, though I learned to ride, of course. The horses always loved the stable hands more than they loved me, but I suppose that's only fair." She sticks a new dried-fruit ear on Cuddle-Lump. "And when I was little, Amma had the sweetest dog. A big wolf of a creature called Snarlie, but don't let the name fool you. I don't think he barked a day in his life."

Ela gasps a little. "My brother has a stuffed animal named Snarlie Junior. Our neighbour Ms Ambika gave it to him. She said it looked like a real dog she once had."

The Princess is only half-hearing Ela. Because she can't have said what the Princess thinks she said. "Brother? Did you say you have a brother? How ... how old is he?"

"He's seven."

"Seven years old! King's truth, that's quite some time. And how old are you, precisely?"

"Twelve and a half. I'm kind of tall for my age."

"Are you?" The Princess is seeing spots, though maybe it's from the glare of the afternoon sun on the Snow. Or maybe not. "Please tell me more about your brother."

"I don't know. He loves to ski, and he got all the athletic ability in the family. And he loves to burp. My mom showed him how to burp on demand, which turned out to be a terrible idea, because he's really good at it. Other than that, though, he's pretty nice for a little brother. His name is Akash."

"Ela and Akash. Earth and Sky."

"That's just what my grandmother says."

"Your grandmother is still alive?" asks the Princess.

"My mom's mom isn't, but my dad's mom is. Dadiji. She speaks Hindi. And I guess you do too?"

"Hindi? You mean the Naming Language?"

"Um, names can be in any language," says Ela.

"Of course they can. But many generations ago, the Traders brought back books of names, and those were thought to be the most beautiful. So, do you have any other siblings?"

"No, that's it. My parents say they have their hands full already. They won't even let Akash get a guinea pig no matter how hard he begs."

"Yes, well, with the Earth and the Sky, what more do you need?" says the Princess.

"Don't forget me!" says Cuddle-Lump.

Looking clear-eyed at her crumbling kingdom and listening to Ela, the Princess can't deny the years that have passed. Years of eating enough but not well. Years of sleeping, also not well, but enough. Years of digging. Long enough for a new cousin to be born and grow into a child who loves skiing and creatures called "guinea pigs" and is perhaps not bright enough to realize that most pigs are not ideal pets. Frankly, the Princess even has serious doubts about her sled-pig.

All this time, the Princess has been alone, waiting for someone, anyone to return. Technically, yes, even though she chooses to live in the cottage, she sees the King from time to time, bringing him sufficient provisions and news of her progress. He tells her she got them into this mess, and she must get them out of it. He reminds her that they are still royalty. She still has a kingdom to inherit if she can dig her way to forgiveness.

Maybe it's better that she didn't know how much time was passing, that while she was battling Snow and loneliness, Auntie Nithya was focused on her new family, not giving the Princess a second thought. If the Princess had known, she might not have been able to keep going. But now that the Princess understands all she's lost, she isn't going to waste another minute.

"Can you slow down?" says Ela. "You're going really fast."

"Could you please speed up? You're going quite slow." The Princess hears echoes of Madame Vidya's crisp tone in her voice, which pleases her immensely.

"I'm being careful because I don't want to fall."

"Ela, as you may have noticed, there are Hounds, and it's rather cold out here, especially for a Str— someone not from Mistmir. If you would hike at a reasonable speed, not only would you stay warmer and safer, we would reach our destination faster. Frankly, this part of the journey is not that hard."

Ela stops so suddenly, the Snow screeches.

"I am so sick of people who have it easy telling me things are 'not that hard'. Guess what? I'm glad it's easy for you, but not everyone is that lucky."

The Princess doesn't turn around. She tries not to calculate how many days she has been digging, how many cups of melted Snow-water tea she has drunk alone. "Lucky? You think I'm lucky?"

"You're a *princess*." Ela says the title like a curse.

"Hmm..." Deep breath. Stand straight. Questions with

questions. "Has it ever occurred to you that you are the lucky one?"

"Compared to a smart, pretty, athletic Princess? No, not really."

"You do have your mother's love."

"What does my mom have to do with how fast I hike down this hill?" huffs Ela. "I really am sorry your mom died when you were a baby. Really, I am. But you don't know the first thing about my mom. Sure, she loves me. But what she really cares about is—" Ela's voice breaks. She glares at the Princess.

"Yes?" says the Princess, her breath a soft cloud.

"Not me," finishes Ela.

After years and years of having Auntie Nithya to raise and love her, Ela doesn't even appreciate the truth. "I think I see your friend's point," says the Princess. "You are a very slow girl in more ways than one."

34

Ela

THE FOOTBRIDGE

The Princess is smirking at Ela, and Ela is quite sure the burning in her belly is hate. Not embarrassment or sadness or frustration, but actual *I-would-happily-toss-you-down-a-mountain* hate.

Why did she ever think she might actually like the Princess? And why does her mom care so much about a mean, mean girl? So what if her mom lived here once when everyone loved the Princess just because she was a princess? Her mom should know better.

"I don't even know what I'm doing here with you." Ela chokes out her words. She would like to say much, much worse.

The Princess steps back and sweeps her arms out, motioning to the whole mountain. "Feel free to go. Any way you'd like."

Ela splutters. They both know Ela is stuck. And the Princess's smile is full of life and fury. She's enjoying Ela's predicament. Ela kicks the Snow so hard it screeches. The Princess starts hiking at her speedy Princess pace with her perfect Princess posture. Ela would sooner lick the Snow off the bridge to the castle than ask her to slow down again.

The Princess glances back. "Will you be joining me?" she says, still smirking.

The anger that started in Ela's belly has spread to her limbs. She's tight as a spring.

"Surely you don't want to stand on the hillside forever," says the Princess.

Fine. If the Princess wants Ela to move, she'll move.

She bolts. The motion courses through her body, and her feet pound out her anger. Her hood falls back, and the wind catches her hair as she heads down, down the hill toward the icy ribbon of the Meander River. The footbridge is coming closer now, but her body veers away. She twists herself toward it as her head starts spinning. Her legs are still trying to run when she falls.

When she lands, she feels solid, not liquid. She is on the bridge. She made it on. The whine of the Princess's footsteps is behind her. *For once,* thinks Ela, *I beat her.*

Spots cloud Ela's vision, but her mittens find the railing. She pulls herself up. The Princess shouts something, but Ela can't process what she's saying. And she's not going to ask the Princess to repeat it. She's not going to ask the Princess for anything ever again. There's a buzzing in Ela's side. She puts her hand in her pocket, where the green butterfly is shaking like it is trying to fly away. Or maybe it's Ela shaking? The chocolate and sunapples in her belly are churning, and that's when she realizes: vertigsnow.

Not now not now not now.

She clutches the railing. It holds her.

Then tilts.

Then cracks.

Then breaks.

Ela collapses. For a split second, the Snow cushions her.

Then, like deadweight, she drops through the pillow of Snow and a sheet of ice. She hits the river underneath, a layer of water flowing over a pebbled bottom. Though it's not water she senses most of all, or rocks, but metal, clamping down, squeezing all the air out of her body, drowning her.

35

The Princess

TIME STANDS STILL

When Ela falls into the river, time stands still. When the Princess pulls her out, it starts again.

The Princess reaches under Ela and lifts. It's not easy – the Princess's arms are drenched and half-numb, and Ela is thrashing this way and that – but after years of digging, the Princess has nothing if not upper body strength. Ela's out of the water now, hyperventilating and floundering as the Princess drags her up the castle-side riverbank. Ela's flailing madly, but she is moving and breathing, and that is all that matters. By the time they reach the path, Ela is as limp as a rag doll Amma once made.

"Let me help you stand," says the Princess.

Ela coughs and weakly pushes her away. The Princess can't tell if Ela is in shock, angry, or simply not in control of her muscles, but this will not do.

"I'm sorry, and you are welcome to be mad at me when

we are inside in front of a raging fire. Right now, though, we need to get warm as quickly as possible," says the Princess through chattering teeth.

Ela blinks a few times, her eyes bleary and dazed, and lets the Princess help her to her feet. The Princess half-carries, half-drags her to the nearest castle entrance. It's only when the Princess is pushing the door open that she realizes Cuddle-Lump is at her heels.

"Don't forget me!" it says.

The Princess gives the sled-pig a sidelong glance as the warmth of the castle air spills over her.

"As if we could."

Part Five

In the Castle of the King

36

The Princess

RETURN TO THE RIVER ROOM

The Princess guides Ela to the nearest bedroom. Ela slumps against the wall and coughs while the Princess's numb fingers struggle with the sticky knob. It's been years since she's been in this room, but like the other rooms in the castle, it should have dry blankets and supplies to light a fire. The Princess wipes her damp hands on the stone wall and turns the knob again. It gives. It's only then, as she peeks inside, that she realizes her mistake.

She's taken Ela right back to her room – the River Room. It's where Ela stayed her whole time in Mistmir, along with Auntie Nithya and Uncle Neel. The Princess momentarily considers dragging Ela away and taking her to some space that doesn't hold so many memories. But Ela can't seem to stop shivering. They may be inside, but the cold is still a danger.

"After you," says the Princess.

Ela shuffles inside. She drops her drenched mittens on the floor and sits on the bed. She slowly stretches and bends her fingers, and coughs again. She peels off her coat and tugs at a boot. It comes off with the snowshoe still attached. She gropes at a wet sock until it starts to come loose. She breathes heavily, as if even that is taking all her energy. Hopefully, this means she will have none left for remembering.

The Princess takes a quick look outside the room to check for Hounds. She finds only Cuddle-Lump, who she guides inside. She turns to warming the room. To her relief, the tinderbox is full of flame paper, matches, and wood that has had years to dry. The Princess's hands have gone from numb to itchy, but they're steady enough to start the potbelly stove and a fire in the fireplace. She aims the stove's vents at the bed. Her sleeves drip cold river water. The Princess had thought the river might have frozen solid under the Snow, but there was water flowing, enough to mix Mistmir's with the Beyond Lands'.

The Princess takes off her coat and lets herself soak up the warmth of the fire. Behind her, Ela's teeth chatter loudly.

"Be sure to take off everything that's wet," the Princess says. "It all needs to dry. You can get warm under the blankets. If you want more quilts, I'm sure there will be extras in the armoire."

"You're w-w-wet t-too," says Ela.

“Not nearly as wet as you, but yes, I need to change also. Can you promise me you’ll stay in this room and not go anywhere until I return?”

Ela’s eyes widen. “Hounds?” She coughs.

The Princess hesitates. The King does like to keep one with him. She nods. “That plus the cold. I’ll come back, and we can sort out your clothes. For now, though, just let yourself warm up and recuperate. Relax – this is your room.”

37

The Princess

UNWANTED GIFTS

It's Ela's room whether she knows it or not. It's the place the Princess would go to visit Ela before breakfast or to read a story to her before bed. And it's the first place the Princess ever laid eyes on her cousin.

The Princess remembers that day more clearly than any she spent digging.

It was a fall day, just after the Harvest Festival. By this time, Auntie Nithya had been gone for over three years, and the Princess had long given up reading her aunt's letter every night before bed or checking the docks each morning to see if she'd returned. The Princess often thought of her time building the sled her aunt had given her, but the King seemed to have forgotten it completely. In her aunt's long absence, Lord Hesketh alone had the King's ear. The Princess was left to eavesdrop and spy, though she preferred the term "listen and learn".

What she had learned lately was that in addition to

questionable advice, Lord Hesketh was giving her father questionable gifts. The Princess had recently caught a glimpse of a set of teeth from a shark that must have been ten times the size of the biggest fish in the Meander River and the shining edges of a stack of small blades. The teeth may have been a curiosity, but what was the excuse for the blades?

That morning, she decided it was time to break her own rule about not bothering the King. She found him at breakfast, before his advisers had come in for the day. After greeting him, she worked up her nerve.

"Pardon me, sir, but I believe Lord Hesketh gave you some fascinating new gifts. I was wondering if I might have a look sometime?"

The King coughed. He took several sips of tea. "A gift? A gift from Hesketh?"

"Yes, sir. I thought— Though perhaps I'm mistaken," said the Princess.

"A gift from Hesketh?" he said again. "I must have misplaced it." He took a large bite of flaky pastry.

The Princess nodded and poured herself some juice. The etiquette lessons on unwanted gifts. That had to be it.

When given an unwanted gift, smile graciously, send a neatly penned note of thanks, and dispose of it at your convenience. If asked to display it, blame absentmindedness and claim you misplaced it.

❄ ❄ ❄

That afternoon, after her lessons with Madame Vidya, the Princess had a sitting-fitting. First, she had to sit for the Royal Artist so he could draw sketches that would be the basis of any official images of her over the next year, from the cover of the Book to any paintings done of her family. Then, the tailor came in to take measurements for her dress for her thirteenth birthday coming up in two months' time. While the Princess always found sitting-fittings boring at best, the artist's and tailor's comments about she was "growing into an enchanting young lady" and "looking just like a princess should" made this one particularly unpleasant. In their comments, she sensed a pile of unwanted expectations that left her even more unsettled than she already was.

As soon as she was finished, she threw on a light cloak and left the confines of the castle. Along the river, the Kingdom was starting its preparations for winter, and the harbour was busy with boat crews retiring their vessels for the season. A crowd watched as Traders hoisted a small ship out of the water. Further down the bank, a fisherwoman flipped over a small rowboat. Like the hulls of all boats, this one went from clean to dirty without warning, the top half the shiny yellow-orange of a fresh-picked sunapple, the bottom half the dull brownish-green of water-mosses, mud, and even a few cove slugs. The fisherwoman picked one off, and it wriggled back into the water.

The Princess walked on. Soon she was on the path between the other side of the castle and the Royal Slope. She glanced up at the afternoon sun. She could make it up to the Royal Ridge and back if she was fast, and she always was. She had almost reached the iron footbridge when John Hesketh emerged from the eaves, flanked by his brothers.

"Oh look, it's the Princess," said John. He smirked in a way that made the Princess want to pull her cloak around her. "It's never too late to become better acquainted."

"We should get back to the docks," said Joey Hesketh.

"No, I want to go with the Princess," said little Jeremy, who appeared to be growing into a smaller version of his worse brother.

To the Princess's left was the footbridge. To her right, a side door that led to the guest quarters of the castle. In front of her, the Heskeths. So she'd take the rest of her walk in the corridors of the castle. It was a small price to pay for peace.

"Please excuse me, but I'm going somewhere you're not allowed to follow," said the Princess.

"Not yet," said John, with a smile as cold as the winter that was lying in wait.

38

The Princess

THE SURPRISE

As soon as the door shut behind her, the Princess started shaking. It was beyond illogical to be so upset; the only thing worse would be if someone saw her in this state. She slipped into the antechamber of the nearest bedroom to collect herself. Before she had reached the bedroom door, she was wrapped in a hug.

"Kiri!"

There was only one person who ever called her that.

"Auntie Nithya?" whispered the Princess.

"It's me, Kiri. It's me."

It was, but it wasn't. This Auntie Nithya was shorter than the Princess by a finger's-width, and there was a grey hair in the strand that fell loose from her bun. The fabric of her sleeve was thin and slippery, clearly woven in the Beyond Lands.

Though the Princess had spent over three years keeping everything together, a moment with her aunt, and all of her questions came tumbling out: "When did you get back? Does the King know you're here? Are you staying for good? Did any Strangers come with you? You said you'd be back, but you didn't say it would take so long! Why were you gone so long? Did you even miss me?"

Her aunt pulled back just enough to look her in the eye and take the Princess's hand in her own. "Let me start with your last question first: of course I missed you! So much! I brought your Book with me so I could keep up with how you've been doing. Kiri, I couldn't be more proud of you. Let's see ... what was your next question?"

"Why were you gone so long? You didn't tell me you'd be gone so long!"

"I didn't know. Honestly, I thought my brother would change his mind, but he took longer than I thought to persuade. I guess he's been listening to that awful Jeevan Hesketh. Is he still parading around insisting everyone call him 'Lord'?"

At the moment, this seemed like the least of issues.

"How did the King change his mind? Does he know you're here?"

"You know the sled we got for you both? The King insisted on us bringing ten more, which was not easy. But eventually, Neel and his team were able to procure them, and it's certainly worth it to come back. By the way, did you enjoy making the sled together?"

The Princess nodded. She couldn't tell her aunt

that was a lifetime ago. "Neel and his team? Are all the Strangers back?"

Her aunt stiffened at the word "Strangers", and her smile got a touch more royal. "The hydrologists are back. And we're planning on staying at least through the winter. So we'll be here for your birthday!"

The mention of her birthday reminded the Princess of her sitting-fitting. But she didn't have a chance to tell her aunt about any part of her upsetting day. From behind the half-open door to the bedroom came the rustle of covers, as if a dog or cat were playing on the bed. But pets weren't allowed in the living quarters. Auntie Nithya knew that.

"What—?"

Auntie Nithya raised a finger and softened her voice. "Before I answer any more questions, I have a surprise for you."

The Princess felt her brow furrow most unroyally. She had had enough surprises for a month, much less an hour.

Her aunt pushed the door fully open and motioned for the Princess to enter. Inside the room, on the bed under a blanket, was a large pillow-sized lump.

"Eelie-Pie, come on out. Your cousin Kiri is here. The one I've been telling you about."

The lump squirmed and shook off the cover. A little girl with a rumpled dress and curly pigtails emerged. She stood up in the middle of the flowered quilt so that large petals surrounded her.

"This is our daughter, Ela," said Auntie Nithya.

"Our?" coughed the Princess.

"Neel and I married soon after we left."

The Princess leaned against the armoire for balance. Auntie Nithya had a daughter old enough to stand up, and the Princess hadn't known. And meanwhile, she'd been blubbering out questions to her aunt like she was just a little girl herself. She stared into the crackling fire and inhaled deeply. *Royal smile. Posture and composure. Questions with questions.*

"My congratulations to you both! What joyous news!" The Princess walked over to the bed and focused on the little girl to avoid looking at Auntie Nithya, who would know in a flash that the Princess was simply relying on her etiquette lessons. After all, she'd taken the same ones. "How old are you, Ela?"

The little girl stared at her fist and slowly uncurled three fingers as fat and delicious-looking as Madame Mittai's sugar-logs. "Free. I'm free years old."

Three years old!

Ela peered at the Princess. And this examination gave the Princess the most familiar feeling she'd had all day. The little girl tottered toward the edge of the bed and said loudly, "Yump!" to the Princess or Auntie Nithya or possibly the door. Though very cute, she didn't appear to be a precise child.

"Yump!" she said again. She put her hands out toward the Princess and flexed her knees, but her feet stayed on the bed.

"She wants me to jump?" the Princess asked her aunt.

Auntie Nithya looked up from her open suitcase and nodded with an encouraging smile. The Princess took Ela's outstretched hand. It was warm and a bit sticky. "Yump! Pweez!"

The Princess gave a little hop on her toes.

"Nooooooo! Yump on the bed!"

The Princess glanced at Auntie Nithya for help. She continued to shelve neat piles of clothes. "You probably want to take your shoes off first."

What in the King's name had happened to Auntie Nithya? Had she forgotten all her etiquette rules? Not jumping on furniture, beds included, was one of the more basic ones.

"Go on. It's really quite fun. Haven't you always wanted to try?"

So Auntie Nithya had tried it? As a grown-up? In the Beyond Lands? It was all too much, her coming back married to that Stranger and with a daughter and so changed after so, so long, while the Princess had been doing everything she could to be the very best princess possible. And now they were all just supposed to start jumping on the bed for fun?

“Mommy, Ki-wi won’t yump!” said little Ela. She scrunched her brow and gave the Princess a cross look that might have amused her on a different day.

“I’m so sorry, but I can’t. I was never taught how to jump on a bed.”

“Well, then,” said Auntie Nithya. “I suppose it’s up to me.” She put down the socks she’d been holding, slipped off her boots, and stood on the bed. Ela held her hand as she said, “One ... two ... three!” They became airborne together. The squeal of the bed frame and the bouncing of their feet mixed with Ela’s happy screeches, and suddenly the Princess would have traded all the sunapples in Mistmir to be jumping on the bed with them. They landed on their backsides and burst out laughing.

As they caught their breath, footsteps echoed in the corridor outside the room.

“Shhh!” said Auntie Nithya. “Someone’s coming.” With lightning speed, she slipped her boots back on and reknotted her hair in a bun.

And that’s when the Princess realized her aunt hadn’t forgotten the rules of how to act like royalty.

She just didn’t care anymore.

39

The Princess

THE EXPERIMENT

There were two reasons Auntie Nithya returned to Mistmir. The first, she always said, was because she missed the Princess. The second was to assist Uncle Neel and the other Strangers with their research. She was studying to be an actual scientist, and while she claimed she was still a student, that didn't stop her from spending her days at the Strangers' Settlement, doing the Strangers' work. The Princess knew having a fraction of her aunt's time should have been far better than none. And yet, the Princess felt even more aware of her aunt's absences now that she was back.

Little Ela, on the other hand, was always around, bursting in on the Princess's lessons, bouncing on her bed, sticking to the Princess like holly-pine sap whenever she went out. Even Uncle Neel made time for the Princess. The Princess had thought he might be mad at her, since she was the reason the Strangers had been sent away. But he was always cheerful, perhaps because he was always talking about science. At best, their conversations were fascinating, and at worst, they were a distraction from all her royal duties.

Sometimes, though, the Princess missed the days before Ela and Uncle Neel, when her aunt would take her for long walks or tuck her into bed, and they could talk about anything. So, when the day before the Princess's thirteenth birthday, Auntie Nithya suggested a walk for just the two of them, the Princess jumped at the chance.

The snow had come early to Mistmir that year, the first flakes falling a full month before the Princess's birthday. The highlands were covered in white, but the ground by the castle was still clear and neither muddy nor slippery. Though the air was cold, the wind was light, and the sun owned the sky. As they headed toward the Meander Path, the Princess tried to decide which of her many questions she could ask her aunt without ruining the moment.

By the time they started climbing, the Princess still hadn't settled on one. The only sounds came from their footsteps and the rustling of the few brown leaves that still clung to their branches. Auntie Nithya stopped and picked one off. She shut one eye and moved the leaf back and forth in front of the other eye.

"Is something the matter with it?" asked the Princess.

"No, not at all. Just examining the frost."

The Princess picked a leaf of her own. The frost looked just like frost always did. "Is it not made of—" She was about to say "water" when she remembered the last sketch Uncle Neel had drawn for her. "Is this about the difference between Mistmir's water and the Strangers'?"

Auntie Nithya peered at the leaf more closely. "What makes you think that?"

"Uncle Neel drew me a picture of water molecules from Mistmir and from the Beyond Lands. He said something about the elements being the same but not the bonds?"

Her aunt laughed tightly. "Uncle Neel can get very enthusiastic about his research."

"What exactly is the difference?"

Auntie Nithya studied another leaf. "It appears there may be a slight variation in how the lone electron pair operates, which could potentially affect the bond angles between the elements."

The Princess didn't know what a lone electron pair or a bond angle was. She suspected her aunt used that language for precisely that reason. Well, if her aunt wanted to evade, the Princess had another way of figuring out the answers. A more fun way. The Princess could just go see for herself what the Strangers were working on.

"Catch me if you can." The Princess almost sang the words. Then she took off deeper into the woods.

❄ ❄ ❄

As the Princess ran to the Strangers' Settlement, her legs coursed with a freedom she hadn't felt in years, the thrill of naughtiness after endless obedience. It was only when she entered the settlement bounds that the Mists seemed to close in on her, and she stifled a shudder.

The Strangers, however, were busy at work, unaware of the Princess as she approached. The snow had not yet become Snow, and it stayed silent as she walked. Yet there was a high-pitched sound from a shallow box that held the Strangers' attention. The Princess assumed one of them was whistling admiringly at their work.

As she got closer, the sound stopped, and she saw that the box was filled with snow. Uncle Neel leaned forward and slowly dropped his large gloved hand into the centre. He kept it there for several seconds and then raised it abruptly, leaving a handprint. The whistling sound came back along with a smell, like metal. Then his handprint was gone.

What a trick! Clearly, her uncle's hand hadn't really touched the snow, but its shadow looked so much like an actual print. One of the Strangers scribbled numbers in a notebook, while another operated some sort of measuring tool. Uncle Neel carefully cleaned off his glove and put it back on. Then he dropped his hand into the snow box again.

This time, the Princess watched carefully as his fingers sunk into the snow. There was no question he'd made contact. He pulled his hand up again. The print filled in with a whistle, and that scent returned, the same as before. The snow sat in the box, seemingly untouched.

It was in the middle of the third trial that Auntie Nithya reached the edge of the settlement.

"Kiri!" she yelled. "Kiri!" Her voice echoed in the glade, and as the Strangers turned, startled, the Princess realized her aunt might be warning them, not calling her. But the Princess didn't care. She'd just witnessed a miracle.

"What is it?" she breathed.

"Snow," said Uncle Neel. "With a capital S."

"That's just what he calls it," panted Auntie Nithya, who'd finally caught up with the Princess.

Before the Princess could reply, little Ela stumbled out of one of the Strangers' cramped shelters and ran toward the Princess. The Strangers moved in front of their equipment, guarding it.

"Ki-wi!"

"Eelie-Pie!"

Ela giggled. "See? Magic snow!"

The Princess froze her face in a smile. Three-year-old Ela, who never left breakfast without being partly covered in jam, had known about the Snow – and the Princess hadn't?

"It's not magic; it's science. Remember, Ela, we're harnessing the power of fluctuating bond angles." Her father over-enunciated the last phrase like it was a concept he'd been trying to teach her with little success.

"You were supposed to be watching her," muttered Auntie Nithya.

"I thought she was napping," said Uncle Neel.

Before Auntie Nithya could reply, Ela ran back toward the shelter. Auntie Nithya pressed her lips together and chased her.

"What a fascinating experiment! I'd love to hear more. Do you have a use in mind for this discovery?" said the Princess to Uncle Neel, royal smile fixed on her face.

"I'm glad you think it's fascinating. It could be groundbreaking."

"How so?" asked the Princess.

"There are places in my world where there are glaciers – or were, at least. Our climate is changing, and our ice is melting so fast, it's accelerating the change. If we could just find a way to keep the snow on the glaciers' surface, it could slow down the warming. The properties of Mistmir water seem to allow us to modify the molecules so that the snow can replenish itself. And if it does that—"

"Neel is getting way ahead of himself," interrupted Auntie Nithya, who'd returned with Ela in her arms.

The Princess's mind was reeling. "That's why you came back? To use our water to fix the snow in the Beyond Lands?"

Before Uncle Neel could answer, Auntie Nithya said, "We came back for you. That was the biggest reason."

But clearly it wasn't. They'd come back for Mistmir's

water, which apparently could do world-changing magic. "Will everyone in the Beyond Lands want our water now?"

"No one else in the Beyond Lands knows about Mistmir. We've kept it a secret. It's probably better that way," said Uncle Neel.

"And Kiri, we don't even know if this experiment will actually work," said Auntie Nithya.

"But it does work! You saw it. I saw it. Even Ela's seen it," said the Princess.

"It does seem promising," said Uncle Neel with a grin. "Though Nithya is right; we are in the early phases of experimentation, so at this point, we really can't—"

"Can't talk about it anymore," finished Auntie Nithya.

But of course they could. Uncle Neel would have talked about it all day if Auntie Nithya had let him. But clearly her aunt didn't trust her enough.

The Princess was ready to storm off, and she'd have been perfectly happy to knock over some of Auntie Nithya's precious science equipment as she did. But all her etiquette training would let her do was nod curtly and mutter, "Congratulations on your success thus far." She hurried into a stand of sage-pines, their boughs dusted with snow.

This time her aunt caught up with her in a minute. All she said was "Shall we walk up to the Royal Ridge?"

The Princess gave a quick shrug and let her lead the way. All her energy from before had been sapped by her anger and more than a little embarrassment.

"All this time—" *All this time, I thought you might stay.* How foolish the Princess would feel saying those words when her aunt was dedicating her life's work to fixing another land.

"Yes?" said her aunt.

"All this time ... the Strangers gave me flutterbyes, just pretty little toys. And all this time, they could do real magic."

"It's science, not magic. And those flutterbyes aren't pretty little toys; they're pretty little sensors," snapped Auntie Nithya.

"What – what – do you mean?"

"The tube that makes their bodies has a precise measure of water from each land. Not only can you use flutterbyes to pass from one land to the other, flutterbyes can sense passing points, whether they're the more common ones that appear on waterways, or the rarer ones that form in caves or mists. That's how the scientists returned each year – by studying flutterbye vibrations. The people you call Strangers have given you a far greater gift than you could imagine – the freedom to be in whichever world you choose."

The Princess's mind raced, trying to process her aunt's words. It was true; the Princess had flutterbyes everywhere – in jewellery boxes and toy chests, even display cases in the Visitors' Hall – and she'd never given them much thought. But how could she have known how special they were when no one had told her?

"I'm sorry, Kiri, if I spoke too harshly. It's just that..." Auntie Nithya paused. The Princess knew that sound – it was the space people gave themselves before breaking bad news to royalty. No one liked to do that, including, apparently, other royalty. "In reality, this Kingdom is not so big. And the Beyond Lands have so many possibilities. I'm not saying they're perfect, not even close. My first year there I was so overwhelmed by the noises and smells and speed of the place. And it's so large, it's much harder to find passing points there, and just knowing that made me even more homesick. But eventually I adjusted and found myself learning more than I thought possible. And you could too. Just think, Kiri – a world with billions of people!"

The Princess knew the Beyond Lands had billions of people. It was one of the many strange facts she had tucked away, along with ones like there were places in the earth where it opened up and spewed something called lava to make new earth, and there was a fish that became round and spiked when it felt threatened. Indeed, there was no shortage of facts about the Beyond Lands that were interesting, somewhat difficult to believe, and had absolutely no bearing on the Princess's life.

"Everything I could want is here." The Princess motioned in an arc to the Boundary Mists that surrounded the Kingdom.

"I'm sorry; this has come out all wrong," sighed her aunt. "All I'm trying to say is that you have choices, including in the Beyond Lands. And those flutterbyes are there for you if you ever want to leave."

"And I am saying that there is nowhere else I would ever want to go."

"But Kiri, there are so many places you could see."

"Yes, but I'm not a princess in any of them."

Auntie Nithya pressed her lips in a tight line. The Princess knew that yet again she'd said the wrong thing. But for the first time since her aunt's return, she didn't even care.

40

Ela

INSIDE THE ARMOIRE

"Don't forget me!" says Ela's mom.

Ela wakes up but doesn't open her eyes. Instead, she pulls the covers up higher and nestles into the warm spot her body has made on the mattress. She was having the weirdest dream about the Snow Princess girl. They were together in this strange land covered in this almost magical snow, and she was about to figure out something important.

Her pillow is mushy. Wet too. Has she been drooling that much? As she moves to wipe her face, it hits her that this is not her pillow and she's not in her bed. Where is she? Oh yeah, the vacation rental. Another snowy, misty vacation, searching for something they never find. But even with her eyes closed, she can tell from the amount of light in the room that it's day, not night, and something unpleasantly cold is touching her face. It's not until she pushes it away that she realizes it's her own hair.

She opens her eyes and sits up with a start. She's in a room with a crackling fire in the fireplace and stone walls and a quilt with some strange, beautiful flower in the centre. Her dream about the Snow and the Princess – it wasn't a dream. Which means ... whatever important thing she was about to learn about herself, whatever answers she's been searching for, it's not too late to find them.

Late-afternoon light streams through the window. She sniffs the smell of the fire and rubs the embroidery on the quilt, and something tugs on the deepest part of her memory. She's been here before, in this very room. She pictures her parents here too, but she's not sure about that part. It's easier to believe in magic Snow than in her kind of nerdy parents living in a castle, even an old and draughty one.

"Don't forget me!" says her mom again.

Only the voice isn't coming from her mom. It's the sled-pig. Cuddle-Lump has her mom's voice.

"Is there anything else you can tell me?" whispers Ela, even though she knows it's a robot sled-pig. She reaches over and tilts its head toward her.

Buuurrrrrpppp! It lets out a long, rolling burp. And then it says, "Even royalty burps!"

Ela laughs out loud. Her mom doesn't think much of royalty, and she is an excellent burper. Once, after drinking a can of soda, her mom burped the entire alphabet, and though it isn't often her mom is silly like that, when she is, she can usually make it at least until *J*.

Ela tilts Cuddle-Lump's head again.

Buuurrrrppppp! "Even royalty burps!"

She's pretty sure that's not what the sled was originally programmed to do, but she's glad it does.

She tilts its head back and forth.

Buuurrrrppppp! "Even royalty burps!" *Buuurrrrppppp!* "Even royalty burps!" *Buuurrrrppppp!* "Even royalty burps!"

It's like when her mom and Akash have their burp-offs. Suddenly her chest tightens, and she misses her family more than she would have thought possible. It's time to find out whatever she can in the castle and then get home.

She wraps herself in the quilt and stands. She needs a plan, but first she needs dry clothes. She walks across the carpet to the armoire. "Armoire". It's such an old-fashioned word. She only knows it because her mom says it sometimes.

She pulls at its wooden door handle, each shaped like half a heart. As the armoire opens, she's hit by the smell of her attic: mustiness and roses, her mom's favourite flower. She imagines she's been transported by some magic from this winter kingdom back to her home. But the back of this wardrobe is just varnished wood.

Inside, there is a space like a closet on one side and drawers on the other. At the bottom of the armoire are folded blankets and quilts, and on top of it are extra pillows.

Hanging off the rod are silky tunics, pants, and fleece-lined coats, all in a size that might fit Ela. She opens the drawers and finds neatly folded piles of socks, underwear and tiny clothes to fit a large doll or a small child.

She gets dressed and stops shivering almost instantly. The clothes aren't bulky, but the materials are so much warmer than her snow pants and sweatshirt. She reaches for a coat. She gasps.

Sewn in the collar is a hand-stitched label with a fancy, cursive N followed by a delicate *ithya*. Her mom's name! She was here: not just in the Kingdom, but in this castle, in this very room. Everything Ela is wearing was probably hers. Ela slips on the coat and then a pair of socks and knee-high boots like the Princess's. Ela's feet are almost as big as her mom's, and these fit with just a bit of extra room. The soles are embedded with bits of some sort of rock. When Ela walks over to the fireplace to dry her hair, these boots grip the carpet better than her snowshoes ever gripped the Snow.

She returns to the armoire and feels around the drawers with both hands for a comb or brush. Just as one set of fingers finds something bristly, the other finds something papery. She pulls out a fierce-looking hairbrush and a piece of notepaper, curling at the edges.

She drops the brush back into the drawer.

Her father's handwriting is on the paper. He's drawn

two upside-down-*V* water molecules, one with straight lines connecting the two *H*s to the O and the other the same but with wavy lines. On the back of the paper, he's written a list of words under the heading "Fluid Snow":

BOSE–EINSTEIN CONDENSATE
WAVE FUNCTION
FLUCTUATING BOND ANGLES
ELECTRIC FIELD
MAGNETIC FIELD
POLARITY

and then, underlined three times:

<u>ICE CAP REPAIR???</u>

Ela knows what this means – well, not all the words, but the paper. Her dad was here too. The Princess must have met all three of them. How much hasn't she told Ela?

Outside the window, the sun is getting lower, but Ela can't leave yet. She's so close to figuring everything out. She gets the brush and runs it through her hair a few times. Then she tilts Cuddle-Lump's head again. It burps on cue. Then it extends its legs with a squeak.

Clomp. Clomp. Clomp.

It marches toward the armoire.

Clomp. Clomp. Clomp.

It's not stopping.

Crash!

The pillows from the top of the armoire fall, sprinkling feathers down on her and, of course, Cuddle-Lump.

"Really, Cuddle-Lump?" says Ela.

"A gift, especially for you!" replies Cuddle-Lump.

Knock, knock, knock.

"Is everything all right in there?"

The Princess. Ela throws everything back into the armoire as fast as she can. "It's fine, thanks." She coughs.

"Can I come in? I brought you clothes," says the Princess.

"Just give me a minute." Ela picks feathers off herself as she rushes to the door. "Cuddle-Lump is being, well, Cuddle-Lump."

Her eyes scan the room quickly, stopping at the pile of her wet clothes. The butterfly! She fishes it out of her soggy jacket, squeezes out the wet wings, and drops it into the pocket of the coat she's now wearing. Then she rushes to the door and opens it.

The Princess gives a small shriek. "Please pardon my reaction. I didn't expect—"

"My hair to have feathers in it? Yeah, I know."

The Princess's eyes are unusually wide, but she smiles. "Yes, that's it." She picks a few off Ela's head. "There, now you're all set for the throne room."

"You are too," says Ela.

The Princess is dressed even more regally than on the book cover, in a dark-green dress with a matching cloak over one arm. Her hair is up in an elegant twist, and she's wearing a gold necklace, though the pendant is tucked under the collar of her dress. Her boots are polished and shiny. The girls stare at each other.

The Princess blinks first. "You're wearing a coat. Are you planning on going somewhere?"

Ela tries for a casual shrug. "I was cold."

"Perhaps you should rest more. You could spend the night if you'd like."

"No! I need to get back."

"I understand. In that case, we should go straight to the throne room. There's a raging fire there. Actually, probably six or seven." The Princess nods vigorously. "It's positively filled with fire. To be clear, it's not actually on fire. It's filled with fireplaces. So it's very warm."

A talking-too-much Princess is not one that Ela trusts. Even the regular Princess is a stretch. Ela swallows and then, before she can lose her nerve, asks, "Is the Book there?"

The Princess's smile falters for a split second. "Yes. I think so." She reaches over and starts picking feathers off Cuddle-Lump.

"You think so?" says Ela.

“I know so. You’ll find everything you want there.”

“What about the Hounds?” says Ela.

“I just came down the corridor and there weren’t any, but it can’t hurt for you to keep Cuddle-Lump close,” says the Princess.

As Ela reaches for the sled-pig’s handle, she bumps its head, tilting it.

Buuurrrrppppp! “Even royalty burps!”

The Princess’s mouth drops open. She locks eyes with Ela. For a moment, neither of them says anything. Then the Princess plasters on her fake smile and says, “Let’s go. It’s time.”

And Ela can’t disagree with that.

41

Ela

THE THRONE ROOM

The castle corridor feels a little bosie-doodle under Ela's feet, like phantom Snow. Physically speaking, she knows it's solid stone, but she's wobbly. She holds tight to Cuddle-Lump's handle as she creeps down the long hallway. The Princess trails behind her.

Soon the hallway widens, and the frosted windows on each side of her are replaced by portraits. Her art teacher once said that powerful people have their portraits painted so they will never die. "But don't they die anyway?" Ela responded. Kavi told her she was missing the point, but Ela doesn't think so. Has this paint and canvas kept any of these people alive?

"Don't forget me!" says her mom. Or, really, Cuddle-Lump.

Ela jumps. It's too weird, hearing her mom's voice from this sled-pig. Her mom is not here.

Except that when Ela looks up, she is.

It's a portrait of her mom, not the actual person. Technically, the painted version might be considered prettier: her hair is all black, her skin is perfectly smooth, and her slightly crooked front teeth have been painted as if they're straight. But she's frozen. She's not someone who would laugh or burp at will or get teary after reading a book she refuses to talk about. To the side of the portrait is a silver nameplate: *Princess Nithya, Sister to the King, Royal Adviser.*

What?

Ela understood that her mom once lived here in Mistmir, but royalty? There is absolutely no way. Her mom is a completely ordinary mom-type person. Not that she's like other moms. She gets super-enthusiastic about science and how things work, but dressing up and fancy stuff? She hates it all. She wouldn't even let Ela watch princess movies when she was little. She said they were totally unrealistic.

Wait – was her mom actually speaking from experience?

"It doesn't fully capture her, does it?" The Princess is next to her, also looking up at the painting of her mother.

Ela freezes at the Princess's voice, like she's been caught reading the Princess's phone. Not that she has a phone. But the Princess must realize all the things Ela is piecing together: her mom is the Princess's aunt, the one she's been talking about. And that is why her mom has the Book. And why she goes on all these cold, snowy trips to look for the Princess. And Ela is the Princess's cousin. And the

Princess's dad must be the brother her mom doesn't talk to and says "seems to live in a different world". But he doesn't just seem to – he actually does.

Wow. Ela gulps. This is a lot to take in.

"Shall we continue to the throne room?"

Ela nods. She's come this far. It's time to finish the journey. She's risked vertigsnow and Hounds, and now her parents' anger as well – because there's no way she's making it home before they do. She and Cuddle-Lump follow the Princess, left and right, until finally she enters the place that holds all the answers to her questions.

The throne room is at least twice as big as her middle-school gym, though the gym doesn't have a reliable heater, much less ten fireplaces almost as tall as she is. Also, the gym reeks of BO, not woodsmoke. But both rooms look like they've seen better days. In the gym, it's the scuffs on the basketball courts and the peeling varnish on the bleachers; in the throne room, it's the frayed edges of the gold-and-maroon carpet and the layer of dust on the velvety curtains. Being in either room is enough to send shivers down Ela's spine.

At the far end of the room, the throne is perched on a platform. From a distance, it's downright tiny, and even up close, it's smaller than Ela expected. It's beautiful, though. The armrests are carved in a pattern of roses and snowflakes, each with six sides and inlaid with pearly stones. The seat cushion matches the carpet, minus the dust and fraying. An image of herself on the throne flashes through her mind. She imagines Kavi and her snobby new friends staring up at her, mouths hanging open, their Smarties falling to the ground with a *plink, plink, plink*.

"Please, have a seat," says the Princess. It's unnerving how well she can read Ela's mind. Ela hesitates. "Really, Ela, I insist."

Without looking at the Princess, she plops herself down quickly. It hurts her butt, like when a seesaw comes up too fast. She pokes at the seat with her finger.

"The cushion isn't what you'd expect, is it? Why don't you give it a shake?"

Ela glances down at Cuddle-Lump. It steps forward until it crashes into the throne's platform.

"A gift, especially for you!"

The Princess smiles. "For once, our sled-pig is correct. Go ahead."

Ela hesitates again while the Princess moves Cuddle-Lump out of the way, behind the throne. This castle version of the Princess isn't one she trusts. But the cushion is hiding something. She felt it. She lifts it off the chair. When she turns the cushion, something heavy falls out and hits her foot – ow! – before landing on the ground with a thud.

It's the Book.

Her mother's *Snow Princess* book.

The other copy of her mother's *Snow Princess* book. Exactly the same, right down to the lock.

Ela tries to pry it open. It doesn't budge. Just like the other one.

"I told you you'd find what you wanted at the castle. It wasn't a lie," says the Princess. She toys with her golden necklace as she approaches Ela. Then the Princess pulls it over her head, revealing the pendant that was tucked underneath her dress. It's the key.

"Have you had the key this whole time?" asks Ela.

"What does it matter?" asks the Princess. "I think the real question is what are you willing to give for it."

"But you said..." starts Ela. But what *did* the Princess say? That she'd find the key and the Book in the castle, that's all. Ela knew she shouldn't have trusted her.

"My tutor had a saying: 'Fair exchange is no robbery.' Surely there's something you're willing to exchange."

Ela bites her lip and looks down at herself. She's wearing her mother's old clothes; the Princess must have plenty like them that fit her better. Ela's wearing no jewellery and has no money. Her phone, back in the River Room, is completely dead, not that it worked in Mistmir before.

The Princess lets the key on the chain swing slowly, like a pendulum, as a hypnotist might. "Think about it."

It hits Ela like a boulder. "No!"

The Princess wants the green butterfly. She's been after

it this whole time. Ela jams her hand into her pocket to protect it.

Giving away the butterfly goes against every instinct Ela has. She remembers her mom's hand over her own. "This can take you where you want to go; this can tell you what you need to know." And then her mother's abrupt change of heart, hiding it to keep her safe. From what? Or, rather, whom?

The Princess continues, "You've had the butterfly for most of your life, and I've had this key for most of mine. And yet all this time we've both been missing something. We can make it right."

Ela chews on her lip. The Princess isn't wrong. The butterfly hasn't told her why she matters. She still has so many questions that will never be answered if she doesn't act now. She can hear Kavi's voice after pretty much every multiple-choice test. "Just pick the obvious answer. You make simple things so much harder than they are." This is simple, isn't it? Give the Princess the butterfly. Get the key. Read the Book. Go home. Sure, Kavi could have been nicer, but that doesn't mean she was wrong.

Ela knows what she has to do, whether she likes it or not. She forces her hand out of her pocket and lets the butterfly drop. The Princess catches it. She holds it to her face, shuts her eyes, and breathes deeply. Then she slides the key off the gold necklace and gives it to Ela.

"I believe I still owe you a cup of Warming Tea," says the Princess. "Please, read for as long as you'd like. If there's one thing that's plentiful here, it's time."

For a second Ela wonders if this is all a trick. But when she places the key in the lock, it slides in easily and turns with a *pop*. The pages are smooth and thick as cream, the first lines exactly as promised.

Ela reads.

42

The Princess

THE BIRTHDAY WISH

The Princess was born in winter.

It's the first line of the Book. Often the Princess has wondered: what if she'd been born in spring as the flowers started to bud, or in summer when the Kingdom was in bloom, or in autumn as the harvest came in? Even if she were still a foolish girl with foolish wishes, she still might have her Kingdom and the people who loved her.

But the *Snow Princess* book doesn't engage in speculation, just facts.

The Princess knows she cannot come out looking remotely sympathetic. But there are many things that led to what happened, more than could possibly be written in the Book. She won't make excuses. But she would like to explain.

First – and this is always forgotten – she never wanted a grand thirteenth-birthday party at all. Even before she saw the Snow and argued with Auntie Nithya, she said so. She was tired of her party being a show for everyone else: for the King to play the part of the proud father even though he rarely complimented her in private, and for her subjects to revel in a night of free food and drink and then gossip about the royals the next day. The one person the party was not for was the Princess. If it were, when she announced months in advance that just this year, she'd rather not have a big celebration, the King wouldn't have laughed out loud, and Amma and Madame Vidya wouldn't have hushed her.

The day she turned thirteen, cooks worked double shifts to prepare the feast, and every other servant was on duty, either cleaning or decorating. The only three people who spoke to the Princess were Madame Vidya, Amma and the tailor who'd come by to finalize her dress, and they, too, were preoccupied with making sure everything was perfect. The whole day was a reminder of how the Princess would have to face the Kingdom on her own for a party she didn't even want. It was enough to make her feel like throwing a proper fit. Luckily, she'd had etiquette lessons to prevent that.

That evening, it started to snow. The flakes were like falling stars against the darkening sky, gracing the sloping castle steps and the wide lawn beyond. It hushed the entire Kingdom; it hushed the anger in the Princess's head. She watched, mesmerized, as the ground turned from bare to mottled to a smooth white. For the first time all day, maybe all year, something like calm settled in her heart, and being the Princess of Mistmir did not feel like such a burden. *I am lucky to inherit such beauty*, she thought. *I am lucky to even witness it.*

Amma called the Princess down as soon as the first guests arrived, but the Princess pretended not to hear. She stayed by the window in her room for a quarter of an hour, until her etiquette training got the best of her. When she made her entrance in the throne room, it was a blur of the fanciest silk-wool outfits, of never-ending trays of kebabs and miniature tarts, and of course, of fawning people and appraising stares. The Princess searched for Auntie Nithya, or even Amma or Madame Vidya, but she couldn't find any of them in the crowd of well-wishers. After a socially acceptable amount of small talk, the Princess excused herself. She escaped to the children's table and poured herself a large glass of sunapple punch.

"You are looking quite lovely this evening," said a voice from behind her, loud enough that some of the maids in the wings tittered.

The Princess drank her punch and didn't turn around. She recognized that voice well enough.

Unfortunately for her, John Hesketh was never one to take a hint. He came around to face her, flashing his teeth in what the Princess supposed was meant to be some sort of smile but brought to mind a constipated bear. Fair enough, the Princess's smile was just as fake, though, she hoped, better executed.

"Are you enjoying yourself?" she said.

"Certainly, now that I've seen you." He scanned the room, and though it should have been some consolation that he was performing for an audience and not her, her skin crawled nonetheless.

"Let me recommend the ginger-pepper tarts. I think they'll suit you just right." She knew he couldn't tolerate spice. None of the Hesketh could. "In fact, if you'll excuse me, I'm going to search for some myself."

But no sooner had the Princess rid herself of one Hesketh brother than another appeared. The server with the tray of tarts drifted to the exits and out of sight.

"John says he's going to marry you one day," said little Jeremy Hesketh. He was so much like his oldest brother at that age, the two could have been made from copying paper.

The Princess glanced around to make sure no one else was listening and then whispered, "That's unlikely, since I hate his guts. And I don't plan to marry for a long, long time, if ever."

"He hates you too," said Jeremy, stuffing a handful of sweetberry cookies into his mouth. He started speaking before he swallowed, spitting out cookie bits. "And he's willing to wait a long time, because my dad says you have to be patient to get power. If John marries you, he'd get to be King. I don't think that's fair."

"Oh, you don't?" said the Princess, mildly impressed with the boy's opinion, though not his delivery.

"It totally isn't. It should be me. I'm closest in age to you after Joey, who's too dense to want to be King. But I'd do it in a second."

"Why should I marry any of you?"

"Because the King keeps making bad decisions in the name of tradition. He refuses to give the Traders all the things they deserve. No matter what my father says or does, the King isn't budging. But my father says the King might budge on giving you up."

The Princess's stomach plummeted. The Hesketh's' strategy of treating her like a prized snort-hog was nauseating, but she couldn't say it was misguided. Her father wouldn't give up his power, but could he be persuaded to give her up? She'd always thought her father's indifference to her was a well-kept secret, but clearly it wasn't. Who else knew? Everyone at the party?

She wanted to flee to her room and stuff silk-wool tufts in her ears and stare at the falling snow. That, however, was not an option. Instead, she disappeared behind a fluted column while Jeremy got more cookies. She scanned the crowd for someone to stop her blood from boiling or maybe just give her a hug. Even a kind word would do. In the swirl of jewel-toned dresses and cloaks, she spied Amma and Madame Vidya, staring into each other's eyes, lost in conversation. That was strange. They were supposed to be looking after her.

Through a break in the crowd, she spotted Auntie Nithya. She hadn't seen her since yesterday's walk, and she nervously gave her a small wave. Auntie Nithya brightened and immediately waved back. Then she pointed down at Ela, who was tearing through the room, leaving a trail of pastry crumbs and juice dribbles in her wake, and took off after her. The Princess's hand dropped like a wilting flower. Auntie Nithya insisted her biggest reason for returning was the Princess. Yet here she was ignoring the Princess on her birthday. Why had the Princess expected more? Auntie Nithya hadn't even trusted her with the secret about the Snow. And she'd let Ela see the whole experiment. Little Ela, who had just picked a leaf off one of the decorative garlands and was eyeing it like she might actually eat it!

On the throne was the King. His torso was longer than his legs, so even though he was not especially tall, he looked so when he sat on his throne. Lord Hesketh was at his right hand, probably telling tales or mocking the other subjects. Whatever he was saying made the King throw his head back in laughter. A dull ache settled in the Princess's chest. She'd lost the battle for his regard before she'd even realized she was supposed to be fighting.

She turned her back on the party and retreated into the alcove. She was too well trained to cry in public, much less at a party in her honour. Instead, she leaned her forehead against the cold window and let her breath fog it. Outside, the snow that had been so calming an hour before was already ruined, trodden with footprints and streaked with mud and animal dung. It had been perfect. And now it never would be that way again. Just like time – things were good and then they weren't, people were here and then they were gone, they loved you once and then you became an afterthought. In the end, all you were left with was the knowledge of what you had lost.

"Karina! There you are!" Madame Vidya had appeared in the alcove. "We're all ready for the gift-giving. The only thing missing is you." Her tone softened as her eyes rested on the Princess's face. "Please, dear. You know how the King can get when he has to wait."

The Princess followed her without a word. Time for another performance. What if she just refused? What if she just walked through the curtains, out the door, and into the snowy night? What would everyone do? Would they even care? Or would they call for more kebabs and drinks and play another round of songs without a second thought?

"There you are," said the King as she approached the throne. She sensed a slight edge of annoyance in his voice, though perhaps that was no different than usual. "Our people are waiting to see you showered with gifts."

The Princess had a million responses, from *No, they aren't* to *Would you really pressure me to marry a Hesketh one day?* But for all her education and etiquette training, she couldn't find the words for even one. She stepped forward with a small royal smile on her face and, along with the rest of the room, waited for her father's toast.

He raised a cup and began to drone on about the Princess's grace and intelligence. Yet again, Madame Vidya must have written his speech for him. The Princess looked across the crowd. Even though it was filled with citizens from every part of Mistmir, they still grouped themselves by profession and place, the merchants from town off to the right, the farmers from the outer lands off to the left, and, front and centre, the Traders. In the back was the small group of Strangers. Auntie Nithya stood with them as if she'd been one all her life.

"And now..." said the King. "And now..." As he said it the second time, the Princess caught John Hesketh snickering. How dare he disrespect her father? Even if he did sound a bit ridiculous. "And now it is time for the presentation of gifts."

The Strangers made their way forward, Uncle Neel in front, holding a flat, square box with an intricate silver bow tied in the Mistmir style. Auntie Nithya must have wrapped it. The sides of the box were clear, and the Princess caught shimmers of green, of spring grasses and holly-pine needles. Another lovely flutterbye, just like all the rest. What would it get her? Friends to spend time with her? Auntie Nithya to stay with her? The King to value her? No, no and no. No matter what Auntie Nithya said, that flutterbye would get her nothing she truly wanted.

The Princess made sure her posture and smile were perfect before she spoke. "I do not want your present this year."

Uncle Neel raised his eyebrows and nodded. She'd impressed one person at least. "Very well, then," he said.

"Nonsense!" The King stepped in front of the Princess. "She wants a present, and you will give her one. This is the presentation of gifts."

"But the Princess said—"

"Are you here because of her hospitality or mine?" said the King.

"It's fine," said the Princess. "I don't need another flutterbye. I have so many." She didn't care about what powers they might have had or that the greens in the flutterbye matched her dress. The only thing she wanted was the King, and the whispers filling the room, to stop.

To her surprise, the King did stop. He grinned at her – not a royal smile but an actual grin – and said, "You are absolutely correct." The Princess had to work to keep her jaw from falling open as a warmth spread through her.

"What a sign of your intelligence and maturity that you wish for grander things! So tell us" – he motioned to the eager crowd – "what is it that you want?"

It was a test. The Princess knew that much. She was supposed to ask for something splendid, something that would show that even these powerful scientists served her and her family. But in the moment, she couldn't think of a thing she wanted other than to be left alone. And she certainly knew better than to voice that thought.

"What is it that I would like? I am not yet certain," she said.

The King's smile widened, but through clenched teeth he muttered, "Karina, you are royalty. Act accordingly."

She'd lost her momentum with him in front of the whole kingdom. She turned, hoping her subjects wouldn't notice her too-wide eyes, and looked out the alcove window to calm herself. But the trodden snow was no longer calming. It was as messed up as this whole terrible evening.

The thought hit the Princess like lightning. There was something she wanted after all.

Her eyes locked with Uncle Neel's. He shook his head as if he could read her mind. Maybe he could, just the way he'd read Auntie Nithya's heart and the secrets of Mistmir's water. He might have been the most powerful person in this room. But he couldn't change her wish. She glanced at the snow outside the window and then back at Uncle Neel.

"Fix it," she said.

"What do you want fixed, Karina?" asked the King.

"The snow outside the window. I want it fixed."

Head still shaking, Uncle Neel stepped toward her and whispered, "Don't do this. We really have no idea what the consequences could be."

"It will bring back beauty. And it will prevent whatever is happening in your land from happening in mine."

"Kiri!" said Auntie Nithya. She'd handed Ela off to Amma and rushed to the Princess's side for the first time all evening. "This is neither the time nor the place." Her voice wasn't nearly as gentle as Uncle Neel's.

"It's my birthday, and it's my wish," replied the Princess.

"Don't you understand?" said Auntie Nithya. "This isn't some party trick. If we do this, everything could change."

But Auntie Nithya was the one who didn't understand. In that moment, more than anything, the Princess wanted everything to change.

The King raised his hand, and all eyes turned to him. "You have made a request worthy of royalty." The pride in his voice filled the Princess's heart. "Is that your wish?"

"Yes," said the Princess. Her voice echoed off every surface in the room. "Fix the snow. That is my wish."

As her words hung in the air, an unfamiliar buzz coursed through her veins. Power. She'd been royalty all her life, but she'd never been the one in control like this.

A bubble of energy surrounded her, separating her from the crowd and her sadness inside.

"No!" yelled Auntie Nithya. "You are both being completely ridiculous. We are at the very beginning of our research. We don't even know if we can do this. It's not going to happen."

The Princess's words bottled in her throat, and she started to shake. Auntie Nithya was supposed to be on her side.

The King, however, stayed completely composed. "You are no longer royalty. You are a Stranger's wife. As such, you do not make the decisions."

"I'm your sister, too, unfortunately, which means I'm as much royalty as you are," said Auntie Nithya. "I've had the same training, the same lessons. Though the way you've been acting lately, it seems you've forgotten all of them."

"I remember that you always thought you could learn them so much better than me," said the King.

"Well, the way you've been ruling, it seems I was right."

The Princess wanted to tell them both to stop right now, that they absolutely could not have this argument in the middle of her party. But her muscles wouldn't move. She remained just as frozen as the rest of the watching crowd.

"Please, Nithya," scoffed the King. "All those years you advised me, you were so naive. You might know what books say, but you have no idea about what this role actually requires. It's something you have to grow into. You never bothered."

"I never bothered surrounding myself with people simply because they flattered me." Auntie Nithya shook her head at her brother. "Our parents would be so disappointed if they could see you now, bossing people around just to boost your ego."

"How disappointed do you think they'd be to see their favourite child as nothing more than a Stranger's wife?"

"I also happen to be a scientist."

"Then as a scientist, you can work with the others tonight," replied the King.

"Make me."

The Princess half-expected her aunt to stick her tongue out.

"Gladly," replied the King. His lips curled in a smirk. It wasn't a look the Princess saw often, and it made her blood chill.

He nodded at Lord Hesketh, who then nodded three times in quick succession to a guard standing by the heavy curtains. The guard disappeared through them. When he returned, he was holding the sled the Princess and her father had made together.

The Princess blinked. She hadn't played with it in a couple years; when the King had lost interest in it, she had too. Her first thought on seeing it this evening was that perhaps this was a second birthday present. Then she heard the steps following it out.

Clomp.

Clomp.

Clomp. Clomp. Clomp. Clomp.

The Princess's confusion was replaced by shock. Following her sled and the guard were ten monsters. Low and fierce, they advanced in lockstep through the parting crowd, a mix of metal, blades, and teeth. No two were identical, and yet they were all alike.

"What did you do to our sleds?" gasped Auntie Nithya. For underneath their trappings, they were sleds, just like the one she'd made with her father. Only not at all.

"You ... you ... never said ... I taught you how to program those!" spluttered Uncle Neel.

"You taught me how to program them as sleds. But I turned them into Hounds. Nithya, you always thought I was better at wielding tools than wielding power. But it turns out I can do both."

"It's one thing to be incompetent; it's another to be cruel," said Auntie Nithya.

The King did not answer her. Instead, he turned to the crowd with an outstretched arm. "Behold!" he said. "Behold my Hounds!"

"But why?" The Princess heard her voice as if from a distance.

"A kingdom needs defences, especially when it can be broached by Strangers," replied the King. "And my Hounds have been made to defend Mistmir. Step away!" Straightening his shoulders, he seemed taller than the Princess had ever seen him.

The guard who had led out the Hounds retreated. The King pulled a hand-sized box from his pocket and pressed some buttons. The Hounds stepped out, forming a circle that surrounded the old sled. The Princess, still in shock, could only notice meaningless details: how one had a huge number of teeth, how another had metal pincers on its legs. In unison, they tilted their heads up and down, as if they were looking the old sled over.

Then, in a blur of metal and noise, all ten Hounds advanced at once. Biting, ripping, clawing, jumping, they attacked the sled.

The Princess clapped her hand to her mouth. She wanted to scream. But the only sound in her ears was the clanging and tearing of the one thing she'd made with her father.

"No!" exclaimed the Princess. How could he? Didn't her father have the same memories she did? Within a minute, her sled was in pieces scattered across the floor. The King gave a satisfied nod. The crowd recoiled as if they'd been hit by a toxic gale. Lord Hesketh was the only one of them who stayed erect, the barest of smirks upon his face.

The King raised his hand to silence the crowd. "You have a strong leader. A strong leader makes a strong kingdom." He then turned to the Strangers. "Mistmir isn't as defenceless as you thought. Now, are you ready to grant the Princess's wish?"

"No. This cannot be happening," said Uncle Neel.

The Hound with the most teeth advanced on Uncle Neel. It scanned him, openmouthed. It circled him. Then it lunged and fixed its teeth on his shin.

Auntie Nithya screamed. She wasn't the only one.

The Hound reared on its metal legs and retreated. In its mouth hung shards of cloth from Uncle Neel's pants.

The King pointed at Uncle Neel's chest. "Biter might not be so careful next time. Don't make me ask you again. You will grant the Princess's wish tonight." He pressed a series of buttons. One Hound pawed the floor in agreement, and the others followed suit.

Uncle Neel nodded slowly, his face a mask. Five minutes later, the scientists, Auntie Nithya included, filed out of the castle, followed by guards and the marching Hounds. Five minutes after that, the citizens of Mistmir scattered, eager to return to their homes before any more wishes or mechanical beasts could surface. Only the Princess, the King, a few servants, and the broken pieces of the original sled remained in the throne room.

Five minutes after that, the clock struck midnight, and that was the end of the Princess's birthday.

43

The Princess

PRECISELY WHAT SHE ASKED FOR

The Princess woke the next morning to calm. Grey winter light slipped through the crack between her curtains, and a soft, rhythmic hushing lulled her. She thought for a second about whether she had time to roll over and sleep for a bit longer before she had to get ready for her lessons. Except she didn't have lessons, because yesterday was her—

The Princess sat straight up. It had to have been a dream. She climbed out of her bed into the cool of her room and reached for a fleece-flannel robe. On her floor, Amma and little Ela were sleeping on a pillow-mat large enough for them both, unmoving except for their steady breathing. Ela always slept in her parents' room. But what if her parents hadn't slept?

The Princess tiptoed around them and turned the doorknob with care so as not to wake them. She scurried down the hall to her study, which sat above the throne room alcove. Her heart beat faster as she pushed open the curtains.

She gasped.

The snow outside was flawless.

She ran to a window on the other side of the room. The snow outside it was even more trodden than the night before.

This is sometimes forgotten. The Princess clarified her wish so that only the snow outside the alcove window be fixed, and that is all the Strangers did. In fact, Uncle Neel had carefully cordoned off the perfect Snow twice – once around the Snow itself and then again to create a boundary zone. Both barriers were low enough to step over but high enough to keep the Snow escaping in the wind. The Princess hadn't wished for the Snow to cover all of Mistmir, and the Strangers understood. They gave her precisely what she asked for and nothing more. No matter what was said later, no matter how wrong the Princess's wish might have been, she never asked to destroy her Kingdom.

The Princess stared at the Snow as if in a trance. She wasn't sure how long she stood at the window. She only moved when she heard footsteps from her room. When she peeked inside, Amma and Ela were both awake.

"You're not Mommy," said Ela.

"I hope it's all right we camped out in your room. With her parents out, it was the only place she'd sleep," said Amma. She didn't meet the Princess's eyes.

Was Amma scared of her? What a terrible thought.

"Ki-wi, where's Mommy and Daddy?"

"I – I—"

Thankfully, Amma saved her. "I told you, sweetheart, they had work to do, and now they're resting."

Ela pouted.

The Princess walked to her bed and sat. She attempted to fix a royal smile on her face. Her mouth did not cooperate.

"I want my mommy," said Ela.

Madame Vidya said that the ultimate goal of etiquette training was composure under any circumstances. But the Princess couldn't have kept her voice steady even if she could have thought of what to say.

"I want Mommy now!" Ela let out a shriek that would have rattled weaker windows.

The Princess and Amma exchanged an uneasy glance.

"I'm right here, Eelie." Auntie Nithya walked into the room. She had purplish bags under her eyes, and her hair was a mess, half of it hanging long and tangled, the other half still pinned up from the night before.

The Princess let muscle memory kick in. "How are you doing this morning? Thank you very much for granting my wish. I saw it and—"

"Where's Daddy?" demanded Ela.

Auntie Nithya lifted her off the floor and held her tight. "Daddy went home with the other scientists."

"*Home* home?" said Ela.

"Yes, *home* home," said Auntie Nithya. Mistmir would never again be home for her aunt.

"Why aren't we *home* home?"

"I'm staying here for now to try to talk some sense into my brother," said Auntie Nithya.

"The King man?"

"Mmm-hmm." Auntie Nithya pushed the loose hair out of her face with her free hand.

Ela scrunched up her face. "I don't like him. I want to go home."

"I know, dear. I want to go home too."

You are home, the Princess wanted to say. *Or you could be, if you would just let it. The Hounds won't come back if you just listen to the King. And there's food here and peace.* But then she pictured the scraps of Uncle Neel's pants hanging from that Hound's teeth.

"Would you like a present, Ela?" the Princess asked. It was her standard question whenever she was confronted with an upset child.

Ela nodded, clinging to her mother. The Princess hadn't actually thought of what to give her, and she scanned her room, searching for something. There, on her dresser, was the flutterbye box from the night before, still wrapped. She offered it to Ela, who grabbed it out of her hands and started yanking at the fancy ribbon.

"Thank you," said Auntie Nithya.

"I didn't know about the Hounds," the Princess blurted out.

"Of course you didn't," said Auntie Nithya. "None of us did. If anyone should have foreseen this, it should have been me."

"I saw the Snow. Thank you for granting my wish. I mean, I know you didn't want to, but ... it's really beautiful."

Her aunt's tired eyes met hers for the first time all morning. She reached out and squeezed the Princess's hand. "It is, isn't it? It might be the most beautiful thing the Kingdom has ever seen."

44

The Princess

GOOD SNOW, FUN SNOW

That afternoon, mostly alone and desperate for something to distract her from the memory of the night before, the Princess took Ela out to see the Snow. She didn't tell Auntie Nithya, who'd spent hours arguing with the King in his study, but she wasn't worried. They'd be careful.

And they were. They didn't jump in it or build snow creatures. They didn't breach the barriers the Strangers had set up. They stuck their fingers in one at a time, leaving only holes the size of burrowing winter-worms. They watched them fill and cupped their ears to better hear the whistle of the unstable air. Ela was too small to reach the Snow over the dividers, so the Princess had to hold her up, but she waited her turn and didn't complain. Now and then, it would stick to their gloves, and they would sniff the clean metallic scent before flicking the flakes back into the enclosure.

It was maybe the third or fourth time doing this that the Princess realized something was wrong with the Snowflakes, that exhaustion and stress weren't just causing her to see them funny. Their sides were in motion, and they each had seven of them. The Princess watched one flake, then another, then another, squirm, twist, and reach, settling only when they were all connected – until a puff of air or the slightest touch moved them, setting off the whole dance again.

"Ki-wi, are you OK?"

The Princess forced herself to breathe and brushed the flakes on her fingers back into the Snow corral. They landed with a whisper. "I'm fine."

The Snow was beautiful and contained, and a reminder that anything was possible. It shouldn't bother her that it wasn't like ordinary snow. That was its whole point.

Word about the Snow spread. Soon subjects swarmed the enclosure, eager for a chance to make a disappearing handprint. In the evening, the kids that the Princess used to watch play rope-jump came out for an everlasting-Snowball fight. It ended only when the King's guards called for quiet. And late at night, when the Princess was wandering the hall because she couldn't sleep, she watched from her window as the shadowy figures of what looked like John Hesketh and his father filled up their sleigh with heaping pails of Snow.

They took so much that she could hear the wail of it from one storey up. She considered reporting the theft, but was it even stealing if the Snow could replenish itself?

Perhaps the best thing about the Snow was that it gave the people something to talk about other than the Hounds. No one spoke of them. No one needed to. They existed, and everyone had seen them or knew someone who had, and no one had any idea what to do about it. Better to focus on the Snow, which was lovely and enjoyable and one more thing that made Mistmir unique.

Ela was the first to notice the Snow had spread. The morning after the Snowball fight, the Princess took her on yet another walk to escape the quarreling inside the castle. Lost in her thoughts, she barely noticed when Ela bolted ahead. The little girl had run for less than a minute when her footsteps began to whistle. She very carefully picked up one foot and balanced while she watched her print fill in. Then she burst into tears.

The Princess ran over and scooped her up.

"Bad Snow," sniffled Ela.

"No, Ela, no. It's not bad Snow. It's *fun* Snow."

"Fun Snow?"

"Yes, totally and completely fun. We'll play in it together. It'll be great." The Princess hoped she'd kept the doubt out of her voice.

"Really?"

"Really."

Ela rubbed her runny nose on the Princess's coat and wiped her tears. "OK," she said. "Fun Snow."

The animals, however, were not so easily fooled. The horses would paw at the ground whenever they stepped in the Snow. The more skittish ones needed double the sugar cubes and sunapple cores to be coaxed from their stables. Outdoor cats perched on sills and balconies to avoid it. Dogs and foxes tried to outrun the Snow's high-pitched whine, but the faster they ran, the louder the noise. The only animals at peace were the birds that never needed to touch the ground.

Worse yet, clusters of Snow would appear unexpectedly. Supposedly one had sprung up in front of the Hesketh's manor and another in an outlying town known for its yak-oose farms. Though the patches seemed to appear randomly, Madame Vidya was usually able to trace them back to someone who'd played in the original Snow. Nevertheless, there was an increasing feeling, especially in the farming villages, that the Snow might be more curse than blessing. The Princess wondered if she could wish for sublimation – the process where snow is evaporated straight into the air – for her next birthday. She could still convince herself it wasn't too late for that.

The King attempted to calm everyone. In a speech from the announcement balcony, surrounded by his Hounds and advisers, he reassured the crowd that the Snow was just another of Mistmir's gifts. That said, he was mindful of his subjects' concerns, and therefore, to eliminate any threats to his beloved kingdom, he would hereafter permanently ban the Strangers from ever returning. His Hounds were already being trained to attack Strangers on sight. Because he was so evenhanded, he would apply this order even to his esteemed brother-in-law. Auntie Nithya stood in the audience, stone-faced.

That evening, it began to snow ordinary six-sided flakes. The highlands got more, the low-lying areas less, but everywhere got enough to blanket the ground and cover whatever had been there before. The Princess overheard a night guard muttering their hope that maybe this snow would bury the Strangers' Snow and that would be the end of all this nonsense. The Princess wasn't sure whether she agreed or felt insulted. In any event, she was relieved they called it the "Strangers' Snow" and not "the Princess's".

45

The Princess

LOST

The following day marked a week since the Princess's thirteenth birthday. Over the past seven days, the Princess had done everything she could to make people forget how angry and impetuous she'd been at her party. The memory of how she'd acted scared even her.

So when Auntie Nithya asked the Princess if she could take Ela out again, the Princess not only agreed, she offered to take her cousin up to the Gardener's Cottage. It was an ambitious trek, but that was the point. No one else would have taken Ela out for so long. If Amma had been working, she'd probably have just taken her to see the horses in the Royal Stables, and Ela would have come back complaining of the smell.

The girls set out across the Great Lawn. Though the snow didn't seem particularly deep to the Princess, Ela trudged slowly. Every ten steps, it seemed, the Princess had to stop and wait. Auntie Nithya had said she would join the girls at the cottage, and at this rate, she'd catch up to them before they crossed the footbridge to the Meander Path.

As the Princess waited for Ela yet again, she noticed that the snow she was standing in – all of it – appeared to be Snow. She pressed her hand to the ground, and a thin layer of it stuck to her glove. She held it up and hunted for six-sided flakes. It was a bit like searching for a five-leaf clover in a field, though eventually she spotted a few. Well, it had been windy last night. Some mixing of snow layers was to be expected.

She felt her glove vibrate. Flakes were clustering together, moving of their own accord. Zap! A six-sided flake added a seventh side. The Princess watched as another six-sided one changed, and then another.

"Come on," said Ela, grabbing the Princess's free hand. "It's not Fun Snow time."

The Princess, still staring at her glove, let her cousin pull her forward.

The downside to the Meander Path was that it was long and twisty, and it was only a matter of time before Ela would tire. The upside was that it was far less used than the roads in town, and though the Princess stepped cautiously, she didn't see a hint of Snow.

But just as she breathed a sigh of relief, Ela started tugging at the Princess's sleeve. "Pick me up," she said.

The Princess stared up the long trail. She'd already carried her cousin over the bridge. "Not yet, Eelie-Pie. It's so much further. I can't carry you the whole way."

Ela pouted. "My daddy carried me."

The Princess picked her up.

Hiking uphill with Ela in her arms was even harder than she expected. Her cousin wasn't light, and the snow was getting deeper as she climbed. When Ela held on tight, she'd often pull the Princess's hair by accident. When she loosened her grip, she'd often slide down. Either way, Ela's boots banged against the Princess.

"What do you think about not going to the Gardener's Cottage? We could just go back to the castle and have cake," said the Princess.

Ela shook her head. "Go to the cottage. You promised."

"I'm getting tired, though," said the Princess.

"You promised!" said Ela.

The Princess sighed. She put Ela down and rubbed her sore arms. "If I give you a present, will you walk for a bit?"

Ela held out her hand. The Princess reached into her largest coat pocket and pulled out the green flutterbye. After she'd given the box to Ela, she'd found it back on her dresser, missing only its ribbons. Though she didn't ask, she assumed her aunt had returned it. Sometimes, when the Princess would hear her aunt and her father's nonstop arguing or remember the Hounds, she'd have silly thoughts about where she might go with the flutterbye. She'd squelched them, of course. She would never really leave, but she liked how the possibility felt in her pocket.

Ela's eyes widened. "Mommy said it was yours."

"You can play with it carefully while we walk, and then we can decide who gets it," said the Princess. But before she'd even finished her sentence, Ela had started climbing the hill. She waved the flutterbye in small circles like she was holding a Harvest Eve sparkler.

"Be careful," said the Princess.

Ela made bigger circles with her arms.

"Ela! I told you! You have to be careful with it."

"Stop yelling!" yelled Ela.

"I am not yelling," said the Princess. "I am simply requesting that you treat my flutterbye with care."

"You said it's *my* flutterbye." Ela squeezed it hard.

"I beg your pardon. I don't believe those were my exact words," said the Princess. Talking to toddlers hadn't even been a full hour during her etiquette lessons. The Princess was sure entire textbooks could be written on the subject and it would still be a mystery.

"You're mean. Like the King man."

The Princess froze midstep.

"I miss my daddy," said Ela. She looked like she was about to cry.

In that moment, the Princess wanted to cry too. Instead, she whispered, "I'm sorry," so softly she wasn't sure Ela even heard. Though her arms ached, she lifted her little cousin up again.

After three more rounds of walking and carrying, during which they sang songs about monsters who ate cookies and the like, and the Princess promised Ela every kind of treat on their return, the Gardener's Cottage came into view. The Royal Gardens were situated on the land behind it and extended so far back, they disappeared into the Mists. The gardens were covered in snow now, but the Princess imagined how they would look in bloom when spring came. *If spring comes,* said a small voice in her head. She scooped Ela up for the last leg of the journey.

"We did it!" exclaimed Ela, touching the stony wall.

"We did," agreed the Princess, dropping Ela to her feet. She stretched her sore shoulders.

"Now let's go home," said Ela.

"We just got here!" The Princess seriously wondered why she hadn't suggested an outing that ended at a bakery and not a cottage that was closed for the season. "You could at least say thank you."

Ela crossed her arms and stomped. She did not say thank you. The Princess studied her.

"Wait, Ela! You lost my flutterbye."

"No!" Ela stuck her hand in her pocket and pulled out the crumpled green toy.

"Ela! You're supposed to... You're not supposed to crumple it. Obviously."

"Don't yell. You're mean."

The Princess forced herself to keep her mouth shut. She was doing absolutely everything she could possibly do for Ela, for her family, for her kingdom, and it was never, ever enough.

"Go away! Leave me alone!" stormed Ela.

"Why don't you go away and leave *me* alone?" replied the Princess. She didn't mean it, of course, and she's had years to regret it, but it is true that's what she said.

"Fine!" said Ela. She ran off.

The Princess leaned against the cottage and closed her eyes. Her mind was racing, and her heart was tangled, but just as on her birthday, the silence was a gift. At least she was away from her family's endless fighting and her subjects' suspicious glares. She'd even managed to escape the Snow.

She breathed in the cool air. There was a familiar whine in the distance that made her spine crawl. She opened her eyes. She saw nothing.

She closed her eyes again. She was still alone, no one demanding anything. She needed to find a way to make that last.

And that's when it hit her. She wasn't supposed to be alone.

"Ela?" she called.

There was no response. Maybe the little girl was still mad at her. The Princess sighed.

"I'm sorry, Eelie-Pie. It's time to come back now."

Still nothing.

The Princess began to follow the little girl's footsteps as she called more loudly, "Eeee-laaa, Eeee-laaa." A few people came out of their homes or work, but the Princess paid them no mind. All she cared about was the imprint of small boots in the snow that led from the side of the cottage to the snowfield beyond.

As the Princess turned out of the shadow, the winter sun shimmered so brightly that at first she thought she couldn't see Ela's footprints simply because she was blinded by the glare. Even after she blinked, she couldn't quite tell where the land ended and the Mists started. It was only when she heard her own steps whine that she realized she was walking in Snow. That's why there were no footprints. She spun around wildly once, twice, thrice. She screamed Ela's name.

No answer. The Snow glittered like a sea of crushed diamonds.

Ela, her clumsy little Eelie-Pie, was under it. Buried.

"Eeee-laaa!"

The Snow gave away nothing.

The Princess dropped to her knees and began clawing

at the Snow. She threw aside clump after useless clump, but each opening closed before it could reveal anything but more Snow. Again and again, it returned to its original state, taunting and whole. She screamed some more.

At some point, more people came. A few broke the latch on the Gardener's Cottage and brought out shovels for the rest. But even a dozen people digging were no match for the Snow. Finally, after what felt like a lifetime, Auntie Nithya arrived on uphill skis.

"The girl's gone without a trace," someone called out.

"Ela—" gasped the Princess.

"You lost her!" said Auntie Nithya.

It was the Snow, not the Princess. But was there even a difference?

Auntie Nithya didn't wait for a reply. She had already advanced into the Snowfield, her full attention on a small, dull-grey flutterbye she'd pulled from her pocket. Apparently, they worked just as well fancy or drab, because within a minute of Auntie Nithya holding it up and moving this way and that, the flutterbye began to tremble. Auntie Nithya circled the spot until the flutterbye was shaking so hard that Auntie Nithya herself was vibrating.

Then Auntie Nithya dived into the Snow, letting it swallow her up too.

And that is how the Princess lost one or, depending how you're counting, two of her favourite people.

Part Six

Two Princesses

46

The Princess

A MESSAGE FOR THE KING

The Princess hurries down the dim corridor, every step taking her further from the Book and closer to the King. Further from her past failure, closer to regaining her past glory. The castle is large, but the list of rooms the King visits is not: the kitchen pantries, his workshop, his study, his bedroom. The throne room, too, but she knows he's not there. Soon, she will say, *You'll never believe what I found, Your Majesty.* Maybe she'll add, *Thank you so much for your patience, Father.* Would the flattery please him or make him suspicious? Maybe she should keep it simple: *I have good news, sir.* "Sir" works. That way she doesn't have to decide between addressing him as her ruler or her parent.

She knocks softly on his study door. It's silent – no mechanical hum of whichever Hound he's kept with him for the day, no rough clearing of his throat. Next, the workshop. It's where he spends the bulk of his time, though she does her best to avoid it. The door is ajar and she peers in. Advisers used to jockey for position at the same long table that is now littered with the scraps of metal and ceramic fragments he uses to improve his Hounds.

The kitchen is the next logical choice. The Princess turns down the hall, but she's dragging when she should be running. What's wrong with her? She shouldn't be nervous. Her plan is foolproof. The Princess finally has the flutterbye, and Ela's entirely in her mother's clothes. Ela has nothing from the Beyond Lands to let her pass through. She's stuck here. Even the King should be impressed with the Princess's scheme.

"Karina, is that you?" says the King from inside the kitchen. His back is to her as he opens a package of spice biscuits. A Hound is with him. Cutter, the Princess thinks, though she sometimes confuses it with Ripper.

"Yes, sir, I—"

"Ending your digging early so you can have tea? Well, make me some while you're at it. And we're getting low on snacks; be sure to bring more from the yurts tomorrow."

"I actually have brought more snacks. I'll bring them over in a minute, sir. But first—"

"First, you need to put the kettle on. Agreed. It's cold outside, as you may have noticed." He chuckles to himself.

The Princess presses her lips together, grabs the dented kettle from the stove, and fills it.

"Sir, today, when I was out digging—"

"Let me guess. You tried to do something fancy with one of your shovels and you broke it and now you want another." He rubs his beard. He still keeps it trimmed, if not quite as neatly as before. "I'll consider your request."

That's how he is. No matter what Auntie Nithya said about him being happier as a tinker, the King enjoys his power. He likes making people earn his respect. These days, the Princess is the only one left.

"I found the girl, sir," she says. The kettle starts to whine, and she tends to it. "The girl," she says again, more to the stove than to the King. She gives herself a bag of sweetberry-ginger tea, her favourite, because surely she deserves at least that.

"What did you say?"

"I found Ela, sir."

The King explodes in laughter. "Oh, you are funny! Ela here in the castle. Perhaps it's just as well you stopped digging early today."

The Princess hopes there is some actual happiness in his laughter. This was supposed to be a joyful moment. "Sir, she's here."

"Oh, is she? Is she hiding in the pantry? Or nestled in the rafters? Or is she at the entrance, waiting for the Hounds to return for the evening?"

"No," says the Princess. "I've got her in the throne room."

The King's face drops with such surprise, the Princess

wishes she'd already given him his tea, just to watch him spit it out. Of course, she'd be the one to clean it up, so perhaps it's just as well that she hasn't.

He blinks and says, "Are you saying that the girl whom you lost – your cousin – is in my throne room right now?"

"Yes, sir." She pours the water into his cup. The steam clouds her face.

"The daughter of my only sister?"

"That is correct, sir." The Princess fills her cup too.

He nods slowly, and her words seem to sink in because his next question is "Are her parents with her?"

The Princess's breath hitches. "No," she says, trying to keep the disappointment from her voice.

"Then how did she come? The rivers are still too frozen to sail on."

"She came through the Mists, sir. Through a passing point."

"The girl came alone through the Mists and is now in my throne room doing what ... tending the fires? Are you sure you didn't spend too much time in the sun, Karina?"

"I'm certain, sir. I left her in the throne room reading my Book."

The King's eyes widen, and he walks over to the Princess, Cutter at his heels. The Princess holds out the green flutterbye in her open palm. Its wide wings are made for flight. Strange to think of it as a trap.

"This is how she came?"

"Yes, sir. And she's in Mistmir clothes, and besides, the passing point she came through is bound to shift if it hasn't already. She won't know where to leave even if she could." The Princess swallows. "I've planned it all out, sir."

The King stares at the flutterbye and then meets the Princess's eyes. For the first time in a long, long time – the Princess's thirteenth birthday, maybe? – his face is filled with pride. "Very nicely done, Karina. I believe we may get our Kingdom back after all."

Those words are worth everything, more than all the digging and loneliness and lost time combined.

They may even be worth more than the Kingdom itself.

47

Ela

BOOK NOTES

The Princess didn't lie.

Most of the *Snow Princess* book is bosie-doodle boring – what she wore, what she studied, how gracious her last two Harvest Festival remarks were. Ela is skimming, and she could still practically fall asleep. Honestly, if the Princess were this much of a snooze-fest in real life, Ela would probably be back at the cottage, napping. The Book isn't totally useless, though. Ela understands more about her mother's past – for example, when her mom says she can't figure out how to use the remote because she didn't grow up with one, she *really* didn't grow up with one.

Ela yawns, not bothering to cover her mouth. She's too warm in the throne room with her mother's coat on, but it feels like protection against the creepiness of this place. She unbuttons it and turns the page.

"The Lost Child," it says. It starts talking about "little Ela".

Little *Ela*?

There's a chapter about her?

The author of the Book clearly approved of the Princess. Ela, on the other hand, was "a clumsy child, speaking when she should be listening, silent when it was time to speak". Yeah, well, that hasn't changed much. At least she's described as cute as a sweetberry (which, weirdly, is exactly what her neighbours Ms Ambika and Ms V used to say when they'd babysit her).

She turns another page. It's the Princess's thirteenth birthday, and it's time for her to make a wish. And suddenly, nothing is boring anymore. There are vicious Hounds (which aren't hounds – they're machines! The Princess really should have mentioned that. And they attacked her dad! Not OK.) And there's Snow, which her dad basically invented. She hears his voice: "It can be a lot easier to do things than to undo them. It can be impossible to predict the ramifications of your discoveries." No kidding. In the Book, it's spreading like a sickness, and no one knows where it will turn up next.

Apparently not even Ela.

She's disappeared in it.

No one can find her. Until...

Once Nithya was certain of the spot, she dived in like a falcon with dizzying speed and precision.

Without a glance backward, she disappeared from the Kingdom where she might have ruled one day. It was a terrifying sight, the Snow covering her like the sea covers the drowning, and we may never know if she saved the lost child or if both perished. All we know is that she would give up everything for the most precious gift she had: her daughter.

Me, thinks Ela. *That's me.*

All those years when her mom was hiding the Book and dragging her on weird vacations to cold, misty places, she'd already risked her life for clumsy, awkward little Ela? What was her mother thinking as she let the Snow swallow her up? Did she think she might die? How did they both survive? It seems impossible.

Ela turns the page once her hands are steady enough, but there's nothing more about her or her mother. All that's left is a final, neatly scripted paragraph.

After that, the citizens of Mistmir could no longer deny the dangers to themselves. When would their animals settle? When would their crops grow back? And, perhaps worst of all, what of the King's Hounds? All questions and no answers. The Snow swallowed and swallowed, and its appetite never ceased. Outwardly, Mistmirians pretended to believe the King's decree that the Snow was a gift. When children lost their toys or mittens, their parents would comfort them. They'd say, "It's just a small thing." They'd say, "We lose things every winter." They'd say, "Remember what the King said." And once the children were asleep, they'd pack their belongings and plan their escape.

The rest of the page is blank, and so is the opposite page, as if the author, like everyone else in Mistmir, decided they needed to leave.

Ela rests her hand on the smooth page and chews her lip. Something is bugging her.

Only a little bit of the story is about her. But that part seems to be about how much her mom loved her. She should have wanted to read the Book to Ela every night. But instead, for years, she's kept it hidden and locked.

That doesn't make sense. Unless there's more to the story.

She turns the heavy page. Two more blank pages. She turns another.

There's more. Sort of. The ink is the same, but the handwriting is different, and it's not a story anymore. Instead, in large letters are the words:

It is heretofore decreed in the Kingdom of Mistmir that time shall stand still until the Princess has made amends, our subjects have returned, and the Kingdom can be restored.

A nervous laugh escapes her. Time shall stand still? What a weird thing to "decree". A shiver runs up her spine.

She turns another page. There's a note in the same writing.

Nithya, I know you and Ela are reading this. Mistmir needs you to fix your mess.

Nithya, you always thought you could rule better than me. Now is your chance.

Nithya, tell the Mistmirians they should return. You know they'll listen to you. They don't have to be Strangers in the Beyond Lands.

Nithya, come back and allow Ela to be the princess she really is. How can you take that away from her?

There is one note back, in her mother's handwriting:

Tell Karina we are trying to find a way. She is welcome to be with us.

There is a reply in the other writing:

Nithya, if you find a way to take my daughter, I'll find a way to take yours.

Ela looks to the opposite page. She almost drops the book.

Ela, you could be a princess. Ask your mother to bring you here.

Ela, take your flutterbye and find the Mists.

Ela, keep your flutterbye with you. You never know when a misty spot will let you pass through.

Ela, don't you love sunapples? Come to Mistmir for all the sunapple treats you could want.

Ela, your crown is waiting.

Ela, come and be someone. This is your real home.

Ela, in this land, you'll always be a princess.

Ela gulps. Page after page of creepy notes addressed directly to her. She slams the book shut and stares at the cover. Someone – well, she knows who – has been trying to lure her to Mistmir for years. She needs to leave, like, yesterday.

Footsteps sound just outside the room.

She drops the Book. She jumps to her feet. Time is definitely not standing still. In fact, she'd swear it is speeding up, racing faster than her heart. A man with a short beard and a crooked crown strides toward her. It's the man who made the Hounds, the man who tried to bait her to come, the man whose throne she is standing in front of at this very instant.

In other words, the King.

48

The Princess

FLATTERY AND STRATEGY

"Please, please, don't get up."

Those are the King's first words to Ela, and in a tone far gentler than he ever uses with the Princess. Nevertheless, Ela does not obey him. She stays standing, clutching the Book to her chest.

The Princess, holding the tea tray, stays next to her father. For the first time in a long time, they are a united front. She pretends to study the steaming cups while sneaking glances up at Ela. But Ela won't even look at her.

The Princess flushes. This part was bound to be awkward. But keeping Ela here is for her own good. She wants to be special, and now she will be.

"Have you had a chance to read the Book, Ela?" says the King.

"Yes," Ela squeaks.

The King doesn't seem to notice that Ela didn't say "Your Majesty" or even "sir". Instead, he motions to the throne and flashes her his version of a royal smile. "If you've read the Book, then you know that you are a princess of the Realm of Mistmir. You belong here, in this room in this Kingdom. Have a seat on the throne. It suits you quite well."

The Princess stares in shock as Ela steps *away* from the throne. The nerve. The Princess can't begin to imagine her father's reaction if she'd responded to that request so disrespectfully. Not that she's ever had the opportunity, since he's never asked her to sit on his throne. She's done it, of course, but always looking over her shoulder to make sure no gossiping servants or grasping advisers were watching. And here Ela is, refusing the King's invitation. But that's Ela for you. She never knows how lucky she is.

"Please, do relax and make yourself comfortable," says the King.

Ela shakes her head no.

"You've given us such a great honour by choosing to grace us with your presence." The King's indulgent smile hasn't wavered.

The Princess sets the tea tray down on a side table hard enough that a bit of tea splatters out of the cups.

"I brought her back," she says. She knows it's best to let someone else bring up your achievements, but Ela isn't talking, and the King seems to have forgotten.

The King turns to her, his smile stiffer. "You brought

her back, she came back, I willed her back. We could spend hours quibbling about the details."

But the details are clear. "I saw her foot last night when I was out by the Boundary Mists near the High Plateau. I returned there this morning to dig and found her again and spent the better part of the day guiding her to the castle."

"I presume you didn't lead her through the Mists in the first place?" The King winks at Ela, who doesn't even seem to notice.

"I found her! I saved her today. Twice!" The Princess has spent years digging and dreaming of this moment, and she is not going to let it all be for nothing.

"Understood, understood. You lost her; you found her. Shall we call it a draw?" The King turns back to Ela. "Please excuse us for a moment." He turns to the Princess and says sharply, "Karina, this isn't the time."

Time? He wants to talk about time? How many years did she spend searching for a flutterbye or for any proof that the people she lost survived? How many days did she look for the smallest sign that her subjects might return? How many moments did she wish to find even a piece of litter or a lost glove, anything that wasn't Snow? The King told her to dig, and that's what she did.

A knot in her chest hardens. She doesn't need to be celebrated. She doesn't even need to sit on that stupid, uncomfortable throne. But she does need to be forgiven.

This room is making her head hot and muddled, and before she can put her thoughts into words, the King is by her side. He drops his voice to a harsh whisper. "Karina, must you fuss right now? Surely you can see how keeping the girl happy and here is in both our interests. Certainly you could try to be a bit more humble."

"It's not fair." It comes out whinier than she means it to.

"You sound like our subjects whenever something went wrong. Why would their lives be fair? I'm a king, and my life hasn't been fair. This isn't about fairness; it's about controlling what you can."

She takes a deep breath and nods. Her father is right. So what if he wants to flatter Ela or split credit for her return? As royalty, their interests are aligned. That's why they both stayed, isn't it? She closes her eyes and recites the rules in her head: smile, gracious, distant, questions. She's so close to regaining her past glory and the forgiveness of the people she loves. It won't be long now. In the meantime, she'll follow her father's lead.

49

Ela

WHAT MATTERS

The King approaches Ela. His crown is tarnished, and his cloak is worn, but he moves purposefully, with a stick-straight spine. The way he walks reminds Ela of her mother. She has perfect posture too. And then it hits her that this man with the creepy Hound-thing who wrote those creepy notes is her mom's brother. Her actual uncle.

"Ela, it is true your life is going to change. But all for the better," the King says. As he steps toward her, she takes a step back. He stops and she stops. He steps again and she retreats again. She keeps the distance constant until she's almost up against a fireplace screen. She scoots forward a bit so the heat isn't burning her back. The crackling is still loud, though, like TV static. The King speaks over it.

"Ela..." he says. "Ela, haven't you always wanted to be someone special? To be more than you are?"

Ela bites her lip and shakes her head fast. So what if she's lying? She's not going to admit anything to the King.

"That's not true. She has," says the Princess.

Ela glares at her. The Princess looks away, flushed. Maybe she's embarrassed. Well, she should be. Pretending to be her friend and then betraying her. She's like Kavi. Worse, obviously. Kavi isn't nearly as polite, but the only place she felt trapped with Kavi was a birthday party, not a castle in some hidden kingdom.

The King waves the Princess off. "No need to be contradictory, Karina. Maybe she doesn't remember what it was like to be royalty. How people brought you gifts and threw parties in your honour. How they stood aside when you passed, how they hung on your every word. Tell her, Karina. It was wonderful."

"Indeed," says the Princess. She fiddles with the gold chain around her neck.

Ela swallows hard. She knows what she needs, and it's none of that. "I want to go home now," she whispers.

"No!" says the Princess.

"Karina!" says the King sharply. He smiles at Ela, the same weird smile the Princess would make, and folds his hands together. "Please excuse her. She has an unfortunate tendency to make a fuss when she's upset. Though substantively, she is correct. You cannot leave.

Your presence is instrumental to the restoration of the Kingdom."

"It'll only be for a bit. Just until we can get the word out to our subjects that you're fine after all, and they can forgive me and return. Then you can go or stay. Whatever you like," says the Princess.

"Well, perhaps," says the King. "There's also the business of fixing the Snow. For that we will need your parents to come back, possibly with their team of Strangers, and implement whatever solution they've come up with. So the first order of business will be to have your parents come for you."

"My parents have no idea I'm here," says Ela.

"That can be remedied," says the King agreeably. He pulls out a large quill pen, the tip stained indigo. "You will write them a note in your Book, explaining that they need to rescue you from the Kingdom. I've tried writing often, with little success. But I suspect a note from you would be much more persuasive. I've no doubt my sister will check it. She's always been too curious for her own good."

Ela's back is dripping with sweat. She stares up at the high ceiling. "I don't think they can return. They've been trying for as long as I can remember."

She thinks about her parents' disappointment after each snowy, misty vacation. And the nights she found her dad up late in his study, hair at all angles, pinching the bridge of his nose. "It's a lot easier to do things than to undo them, Eelie." He made the Snow, and he doesn't know how to unmake it.

"Even if they did return, they don't have a way to fix the Snow. I don't know why you think they do," says Ela.

"Auntie Nithya tried to come back?" asks the Princess. "When?"

"Quiet!" says the King. "Ela, you raise an excellent question. What makes me think your parents can return and repair our Snow? Perhaps there are some things you don't know about them.

"First, my sister. She almost died for you once; she'd do it again. She'll do anything to find you.

"Now let me tell you a story about a young man named Neel. He grew up in a town in a valley with a set of caves surrounded by cold springs. When he was young, he often didn't feel like he fit in, and he would hike to those caves and observe the springs. I'll wager you still live near them today."

Ela shudders, despite the raging fire. This man shouldn't know these things about her family.

"When he was at university studying hydrology, he first took water samples from there and realized that their purity and structure were different than would be expected. He spent years trying to discover the original source of the water that had carved out the caves. Eventually, when he was a young researcher, he traced it back to Mistmir. He and his colleagues arrived on Karina's first birthday, For years thereafter, they'd return on the cusp of winter and depart each spring, as soon as the ice melted. Your father mastered our mists and waters. And here you are telling me he can't return. His 'science' is more powerful than any magic I've imagined. No wonder my sister chose that over royalty. My mistake in this ordeal was forcing the Strangers to leave. How much more powerful I'd be if I'd ordered them to stay and do my bidding!"

The King talks about her parents like they're wizards or something, not ordinary people just trying their best. And he's using her as bait to get them back. As much as she wants to see them right now, she can't be the reason her parents get trapped here.

"I have a little brother. They're not going to leave him."

The King rubs his neck and sighs. "Very well, then. Tell them they can bring him if they must. We have enough spare bedrooms, I suppose." He holds the quill out to Ela. "Go on, now."

"No way," says Ela.

"You are a princess, Ela. It is time to do your duty for Mistmir."

"She's the Princess, not me," says Ela, pointing at her cousin.

"True, true. She is the more familiar princess. But you would be the favoured one. Think of the story! The lost girl who found her way back against the odds. Why, you might even be queen one day. Everyone would listen to you, indulge you, grant your wishes. Just be careful what you wish for – isn't that right, Karina?"

The Princess looks as if she's been slapped. "Yes," she mumbles.

"Why don't you give Ela her tea? Maybe some ginger biscuits too. Let her relax. Mistmir's tea is unparalleled."

"I don't want tea. I want to go home," says Ela.

"People aren't always the best judges of what they want," says the King. "Look at my subjects. Whining about the Snow, as if the Beyond Lands didn't have far, far worse. And now they're living somewhere where they're nothing but Strangers. Ela, you are the lost princess, returned. The one everyone spoke of. You are finally back where you belong. Don't you understand? You matter here. That is the one thing that sets you apart from everyone else."

Is it why she matters? She's been searching so hard for the answer to that question.

And now, here in this castle in her family's kingdom, she knows.

She does matter here, but also everywhere. Not because she's a princess or survived a stunning fall in the Snow. Not because she escaped or returned. And certainly not because she's any smarter or prettier than when she first set foot in Mistmir, because she's not. She matters because she's her. She's a person, like the Princess and the King, but also all of their subjects, and like them, she doesn't have to do anything special to matter. When she gets home, she'll tell Kavi that she matters, too, not because of her grades or friends, but just because. Kavi might not believe her, like she didn't with the sunapples and weird water, but that won't make it any less true.

Ela glances out a cloudy window. The sky is streaked orange, the start of sunset. "I'm leaving now."

"Don't forget me!" declares Cuddle-Lump from behind the throne. Its legs extend so it is standing.

The Princess bumps a teacup. The King's eyes widen.

The King looks curiously at the sled-pig. "Is that—?"

"Yes," says the Princess, wiping up the tea that spilled.

"It survived after all," murmurs the King. He strokes his beard, refocusing on Ela. "If you insist on leaving..."

"I do," says Ela.

"I have some friends who have just returned for the evening. Perhaps they could convince you to change your mind." The King turns away from Ela and reaches under his robe. He pulls out a remote control of sorts.

Clomp.

Clomp.

Clomp. Clomp. Clomp.

The sound of soldiers marching echoes in the throne room. Only they're not soldiers. They're not anything alive.

They're metal and teeth and blades and the King's worst impulses made real.

They're Hounds. Ten of them, not eight like the Princess said.

Outside, Ela is completely still, but her insides are shaking. Even having read the Book, she couldn't have imagined this. No wonder her father is scared of dogs.

They advance on her, and Ela scans the room. She is quite sure there is another door behind the thick velvet curtains. But the Hounds have fanned out, and they move surprisingly quickly, cutting off any clear path to an exit.

They close in. She hugs the Book to her chest as they surround her in a semicircle. Between them and the raging fire behind her, she is completely trapped.

"These are my Hounds, Ela. Or should I say Mistmir's Hounds? And were you to take your rightful place as a princess, we could train them to answer to you, too, one day," says the King.

Ela gulps. She has no words. To think one of these things almost caught her in the Snow.

"I could introduce you to each one if you'd like. Show you their special features?"

Ela shakes her head fast.

"Well then, we should at least allow them to learn who you are, so they can proceed accordingly," says the King.

He presses a button, and in unison, the Hounds move their heads up and down, up and down, scrutinizing her. She hugs the Book harder.

"They want to get to know you better," says the King.

Clomp. Clomp.

They step forward, tightening their arc around her. Ela inches back. They look her over again. One of the Hounds with fangs opens its mouth. Another with razor claws raises its paw.

Ela was already sweaty, but now, between the fire and her fear, the room is swimming. She feels like she could faint. She has to make the King call them off.

What could she say? Maybe that she needs a break? But he obviously doesn't care about that, considering he's controlling the Hounds. Maybe something about the Princess? He doesn't seem to care too much about her either.

Ela is sweating so much, she's losing her grip on the Book. Then it hits her. There is something he might care about.

She wipes one hand, then the other, on her mother's

coat. Then she holds the Book over her head.

"Make them go away or I will burn this book." The fire against her back is starting to hurt.

"No!" says the Princess. "I mean, please don't."

The King doesn't move, but the smile has been wiped off his face.

"I'm very clumsy," Ela says to the King. "And I'm sweaty too. I could drop it by accident."

"She really is clumsy," says the Princess.

Before the King can answer either of them, there's a buzz from behind the throne. Cuddle-Lump rises and advances.

Ela, the King, and the Princess watch in shock as Cuddle-Lump heads toward them. *Clomp, clomp, clomp.*

It's not slowing down.

It marches straight into the lead Hound. Like dominoes, that Hound bumps into another, which bumps into another.

"A gift, especially for you!" Cuddle-Lump keeps moving.

The Hounds scatter in all directions.

There's a clear path to the door behind the curtains. Ela heads straight for it. The King reaches for his controller to make the Hounds regroup.

"Don't forget me!" says Cuddle-Lump.

Ela reaches back and grabs its handle. She slips the

Book under her coat, rushes past the velvet curtains, and pushes against the heavy door until it gives. She exhales as she and Cuddle-Lump cross the threshold into the winter air.

50

The Princess

FORGIVENESS OF SORTS

In the moment the Princess has waited half a lifetime for, her father practically offered Ela the Kingdom. Her kingdom.

"Karina!" The King snaps the Princess out of her thoughts. He's reassembling his Hounds. "You still have the flutterbye."

The Princess nods and holds it up.

"She won't get anywhere without that. Now we'll just wait for her to realize she's trapped and come back." He chuckles. "I'll get my kingdom back yet."

"Indeed, sir," says the Princess.

They sit together in silence, waiting for Ela to return, their future to arrive. The Princess pokes at a fire, and the King toys with Cunning. The Princess sips some tea. It is tepid, but she drinks it anyway. If she has to wait, she'd rather do it in the cozy space of the Gardener's Cottage. She wonders how long until she can politely leave. That's always the question, isn't it? *How much longer...*

"Am I forgiven, sir?" Even though the Princess spoke the words herself, she is startled to hear them out loud.

The King looks up from Cunning and strokes his beard. "You want me to say you're forgiven? You're forgiven. There. But this isn't over. Neither of us wants to rule over only Snow."

You're forgiven. The words ring hollow inside her, like pebbles in an empty jar.

The Princess walks to a closet by the front entrance. She puts on a coat and gloves and straps on a pair of uphill skis.

"You're going after the girl, then? Taking the initiative?" says the King. "Found her once, you'll find her again?"

The Princess knows she should contradict him, but she's not brave like Ela. "Yes, sir," she says as she buttons her coat.

Outside, the daylight is dim but not yet completely gone. The cold air recharges her tired body, though it's slower to reach her muddled head. No matter – the task at hand doesn't require much thinking. At this point, catching Ela? It's muscle memory.

Part Seven

Ela and Karina

51

The Princess

THE PATH LESS TRAVELLED

The Princess doesn't need Ela's footprints to know where she's gone. Ela could have made her way up either the winding Meander Path or the sheer face of the Royal Slope. One she asked to travel down, the other she almost died on. This isn't hard. And yet...

The Princess stands on the Great Lawn for a moment. On her uphill skis, she could catch Ela on the Meander Path in minutes. But the Princess hasn't been on that path since the day she lost Ela. Going up it would only be easier if you define "easier" solely in terms of physical exertion.

After the Princess lost Ela and Auntie Nithya, she would have given anything to disappear herself. But that wasn't a choice. The King insisted she meet with her mourning subjects. They offered condolences with cold hands and suspicious eyes, and murmured kind, false words.

Soon even that pretence was dropped. The people of

Mistmir chose to spend their limited time elsewhere. They packed their possessions and portable food. They made deals with Traders. Then they gathered at night at the far branches of the Meander River to crowd onto boats to take them to the Beyond Lands. The King sent out guards to patrol the waterways, but in the morning the guards and their families were gone too.

The King claimed he was unconcerned by the exodus; the rivers would all be frozen soon enough. He wasn't wrong. But even though the rivers were impassable and no one wanted to risk their lives leaving the way Auntie Nithya did, the Mists were still an option – for whoever had a flutterbye. After Auntie Nithya's disappearance, everyone understood their power. The Princess might not have wanted a ticket to the Beyond Lands, but everyone else left in Mistmir did.

Once, when getting herself a snack from the pantry, the Princess walked in on a cleaning lady pressing an indigo-purple something into the hands of a kitchen maid. They froze, as did the Princess. It's not that she didn't recognize it, but what was it doing with them in the kitchen? The Princess retreated and asked them to bring her tea to her room. It was only then that she checked her jewellery box and realized that not only was her indigo-purple flutterbye missing, but several others were as well. Her first thought was that she'd rather they'd taken the pale-lavender ones.

Her second was that her flutterbyes were being stolen by someone she'd known for half her life. The Princess never had the cleaning lady punished, and not just because she never saw her again. After the mess she'd created, who was she to stop anyone from leaving?

And leave they did. Every few days, more flutterbyes went missing, and more people. The Princess made a cursory effort to stop the taking – she added a lock to her jewellery box; she hid some flutterbyes in her armoire. But she clearly cared less about keeping her flutterbyes than her remaining subjects did about taking them. Soon, the only people left in the castle, other than the Princess and the King, were Amma and Madame Vidya.

They came to her in the dead of night. They begged her to leave with them. They told her that this was the only way out. They promised they'd find Auntie Nithya if they could, or Amma's family, and no matter what, they'd take care of her. They had a flutterbye – did they know it was her last? Amma even started packing a bag for her while Madame Vidya used her most persuasive arguments. They only left when the King's footsteps and the steady clomping of the Hounds came echoing down the hallway, threatening to trap them in Mistmir forever.

Even as they pleaded – Amma's face wet with tears and Madame Vidya's voice cracking as she pressed the Book key into the Princess's hand – the Princess refused to go. It wasn't just that she didn't think she could leave her father and give up being the Princess: it was that she wasn't sure she deserved to.

The Princess reaches the Royal Ridge in record time. As she catches her breath, she lets herself wonder what would have happened if she'd gone with Amma and Madame Vidya. It's true she wouldn't be a princess. But what of all the other things she might have become?

She turns and surveys the valley below. The edge of the sun has dropped below the horizon, but the last rays still light the deserted town that is her home. The first stars are shining – though Uncle Neel once told her at least one might be a planet. She can almost feel the pull of the moon, ready to rise. And then, outside the castle, a glint of metal catches her eye. She peers more closely. Eleven dots – a larger one plus ten smaller ones in front of it. There's only one thing it could be: the King and his Hound-sleigh, ready for pursuit. The Princess takes off.

Ela has proven that she is braver than the Princess. But bravery can take you only so far.

What matters now is speed.

52

Ela

UP THE MEANDER PATH

Ela may have had a lot of fails today, but she's had some wins too. Finally getting to go on the Meander Path is one of them. It's so much gentler than the cliff face she flew down. And it's much better to be leading Cuddle-Lump rather than the other way around. The sled-pig glides smoothly, carrying the *Snow Princess* book in its open compartment.

Ela makes her way through the trees instead of walking up the main trail, keeping her ears pricked. Though it is darker, each tree offers a place to hide if the Princess comes. Or when the Princess comes. She didn't spend the entire day trying to trap Ela in the castle just to let her go. At least Ela's footprints won't give her away.

In the distance, Snow whines. She scurries behind a large fir with thick, drooping branches and glances at Cuddle-Lump. The sled-pig thankfully stays silent. She counts the seconds, one-one-thousand, two-one-thousand.

The Snow whine continues, but it doesn't get closer. In fact, it's getting further.

Ela starts up the hill again, faster now. She needs to find a way not to see the Princess, probably ever again. The thought makes Ela strangely sad. For a lot of the day, the Princess felt like more of a friend than Ela's actual friends ever did. And she did save Ela both times she got vertigsnow. It's funny, but it felt like the butterfly got vertigsnow too. Every time she was shaky on the inside, it was shaky outside. Well, it's the Princess's butterfly now, because Ela's not going back to get it. The Princess would probably argue in her twisty way that it was always hers. From what the Book said, she wouldn't really be wrong about that.

Ela emerges from the path onto the Royal Ridge. She looks from side to side. The land is open, but with no Hound-monsters or royalty to be seen, though there's a distant echo of small noises. The sky is still not black. On the horizon, the moon rises, full and silver.

She decides to run for it. Her mom's boots grip the Snow better than Ela's snowshoes ever did. Cuddle-Lump coasts next to her. They don't slow down until they reach the cottage fence. From there, the Mists she passed through this morning are in sight. She just needs to get past the cottage, down one more hill, and across the Snowfield. Then she'll be back. She takes deep breaths to steel herself against any vertigsnow.

Ela's spine tingles. She stops. She takes a quick glance behind her, but there's nothing there. In front of her is the cottage, above her, the round, watching moon. Her stomach churns, from nerves or vertigsnow. She places her free hand against the fence for balance and keeps going. Her glove pushes against the slats of the fence, then the stones of the cottage, the paint of the door, and then ... nothing at all.

The cottage door has opened, and she's falling sideways. And yet again, it's the Princess who catches her.

53

The Princess

MELTING ICE-BRICKS

As soon as Ela regains her balance, she yanks herself away from the Princess and back out the door. Understandable, but not exactly wise under the circumstances.

"Ela, wait!" The Princess grabs her arm.

"I'm going home," says Ela.

"Don't forget me!" says Cuddle-Lump.

"Ela, you can go home, but not right this second, because the King is out searching for you on his Hound-sleigh, and we can't let him catch you," says the Princess.

Ela stops and looks the Princess dead in the eye. "He sent you after me, didn't he?"

"Yes, but can you trust me anyway?"

Ela snorts. "Um, no."

The Princess flushes. It was a stupid thing to ask. More questions aren't always the answer. "Look, Ela, I expect you'll hate me forever for wishing for this Snow and then losing you in it—"

Ela wrinkles her nose. "You think that's why I'd hate you?"

Of course. It's why everyone does. "You read the Book," says the Princess.

"Yeah… Have you?"

The Princess's gaze drops. "Not in its entirety, no. There are parts that are painful enough to remember."

"It was an accident. You tried to get me back. You were screaming and clawing at the Snow, and they had to pull you away."

That is true. The Princess did all of that, and none of it worked.

"But you're furious with me. Since the throne room, it's been written all over your face," says the Princess.

"Not because of what you did then. Because of what you're doing now."

Ela's words hit the Princess straight in the chest. This whole day, the Princess thought she was fixing the past, not ruining the present.

She drops Ela's arm and steps back. "You can go if you want. You need to understand, though, you probably won't be able to leave where you came in. The movement of the Mists causes the passing points to shift, and it can take time to find another one. I truly think it would be safer for you to hide here until the King returns to the castle. But it's your choice. Either way, I am truly sorry for everything, and especially today."

Ela chews on her lip and studies the Princess for what seems like forever but in reality is probably just a few seconds. Then she steps inside the cabin.

"What about Cuddle-Lump?"

"If we forget it, it will be sure to tell us." The Princess angles the sled-pig inside and gives it a sharp tug forward.

"At your service!" it says, sliding backward.

"Not now, Cuddle-Lump," says the Princess.

She pulls the sled-pig again, more gently. Then she shuts the door and slides a wooden bench in front of it.

The girls tiptoe to the back of the cabin. They don't light a lantern, but the moonlight through the ice-bricks is enough to guide them. The Princess pushes three large boxes away from the back wall, leaving just enough space for her and Ela. They sit shoulder to shoulder behind the boxes. Cold air leaks through the back door. In the dark, not looking at Ela, it's easier for the Princess to say what needs to be said.

"When you go back, will you tell Auntie Nithya – I mean your mother – that I'm still working to earn her forgiveness?"

"Why do you need her forgiveness? I don't think she's mad at you."

"Well, she would have every right to be." The Princess lets her eyes rest on the dark ceiling.

"I think maybe what you really need is not someone else's forgiveness, but to forgive yourself."

The Princess's breath catches, and she shakes her head. "I can't stop remembering all the bad things I've done."

"I don't think it's about forgetting what you've done wrong. I think forgiving yourself is about letting yourself live in the future instead of dwelling in the past."

"I—" the Princess starts. *I have been dreaming about the future all this time*, she wants to say. But has she? The future she's pictured has always mirrored her past. She crosses her arms, hugging herself.

"I was so jealous of you," says Ela. "Every night my mom would look at your Book. And my parents would be whispering about you, and our neighbours too – I call them Ms V and Ms Ambika – but I think they're your tutor and nanny. It was clear everyone cared about a girl who wasn't me. And then we'd go on all these snowy, misty vacations, where they'd explore and I'd just want to be on a beach, playing in the waves and making sandcastles."

It's so much to believe that all this time, the people she loved loved her right back. The Princess's heart beats in her throat. "What's a beach like? An ocean beach?' she whispers.

Ela's shoulders relax in the dark. "It's awesome. The best moment is when you first get there, and you smell the beach air. People say it smells salty, but it's more than that. You know how life first started in the sea? When you breathe in that air, it's like you've come back to where you belong." The Princess closes her eyes and tries to imagine such a scent. "And the sound of the waves, sometimes it's a soft swishing and sometimes it's a loud roar, and—"

The sound is in the Princess's ears – almost a roar but too high-pitched, so it's more of a shriek. In a split second, the Princess realizes it's not her imagined ocean but sounds of the Snow as the Hounds rush through it to the cottage. They stop outside the door.

The Princess kneels so she can see over the boxes. Orange torchlight glows through the ice-bricks. The King hits the door three times.

Bang. Bang. Bang.

"Princess Karina, this is no time for games. Open the door immediately and bring out the Book and the girl."

The Princess can feel Ela shaking. The Princess lays a hand on her shoulder and whispers, "He's bluffing. I'll say you're not here. We'll wait him out, and then we can make a plan to get you home."

"I'm done waiting," says the King. "A girl has grown from a toddler to a near-teenager in the time I've spent ruling over an empty land."

The orange glow focuses on one ice-brick. It starts swimming before the Princess's eyes. The Princess steadies her voice, as she's been taught, and calls out. "What makes you think the girl is here, Father? Perhaps you should continue your search so you don't waste any more time."

The King pauses. Both girls stay stock-still. Even the Hounds stop their growling.

The King is going to leave, the Princess thinks. *He is. And then I will help Ela find a passing point. And then, maybe tomorrow, I will think about what Ela said about living in the future.*

The orange light fades. The King must be stepping back. The Princess can hear the King click his controller, the Hounds marching away from the cottage. She exhales slowly.

"Don't forget me!"

Cuddle-Lump! No!

"You wouldn't happen to be lying to me, would you, Karina?" says the King.

The orange glow sharpens again, focusing on a single ice-brick.

The Princess presses her lips together. Ela gulps. The Princess elbows her to be quiet. The ice-brick is melting, dripping down the wall.

"If you'd rather I burn the place, I can. The flame would melt the ice-bricks and burn the door, but the stone would likely only crack. You would probably come out unscathed, as would the girl who you claim is not there. Probably."

There's only a hole now where the ice-brick was. The King laughs right through it.

"The gossips always said you were quite the thinker. So I'll give you two minutes to think about it before I torch the door. If you're as smart as they said, it shouldn't take you half that time." There's a clatter – the Hounds jumping against the cottage, barking up a storm. The King laughs again.

The Princess is smart, smart enough to know she is trapped. She will need to face the King in a matter of seconds. Time passes here, after all.

But ... but ... though she is stuck, Ela is not. She has a way home. Just not the way she came.

Ela is a statue next to her. She isn't moving or speaking, and she seems to be rationing her breaths.

"I have an idea," the Princess whispers.

Ela's eyes widen. She doesn't answer.

"There's another way back to your land."

Ela furrows her brow.

"It worked for you the last time you left Mistmir."

Ela shakes her head fast. The King starts counting down from sixty. A minute has already passed.

"The Ice Marker out back," whispers the Princess. "It's on the exact spot where we lost you and your mother. It's fenced in, so the Hounds won't be able to get to you. We know the passage is safe now since you made it through last time, and because it goes down through solid ground, it should let out in the same place every time. Usually, to pass through, you'd need something from this land and something from that one, like the rhyme says. But this flutterbye counts as something from both. Sneak out back and I'll make a distraction."

"But you—" protests Ela.

"Please don't worry about me. Just leave while you can. Only, do you know where you'll end up if you make it through?"

Ela nods quickly. "The caves near my home. I'm almost sure from what the King said. And I remember my dad telling me Mom and I got lost there when I was little."

"Twenty seconds," yells the King.

"Go!" says the Princess, pressing the flutterbye into Ela's hand, and then, before she can stop herself, "Please tell Auntie Nithya I miss her."

She unlatches the back door, and Ela slips outside.

The Princess rushes to the cottage entryway and waits next to Cuddle-Lump. She takes the Book from the sled-pig's main compartment and tucks it under her coat. What a day she and Cuddle-Lump have had! She tightens her grip on its handle in case it decides to crash or do something random.

Although maybe not everything it does *is* completely random. All of those crashes were followed by it calling out "a gift especially for you" ... And it only seemed to burp after its head tilted ... And maybe there's a command for something else Cuddle-Lump does...

"Five ... four..."

The Princess pushes aside the bench and moves the sled-pig so it is facing her with its back to the door.

"Three ... two..."

She keeps her grip tight.

"One..."

She opens the door and gives the sled-pig's handle the hardest yank she can. It goes careening backward, right into the King.

"At your service!" it cries. "At your service!"

The King goes flying into the Snow. His torch lands flame-end down and extinguishes with a sizzle. The Hounds are barking like mad, and he holds out his controller, aiming for his lead dog, Cunning. The Princess isn't sure what he has planned for them, and she doesn't intend to find out.

She grabs his hand. He grips his controller tighter, but she's not trying to take it, exactly. She is just going to help him aim ... instead of at Cunning, straight at the very first sled on the network, Cuddle-Lump. The Hounds can learn from it instead.

Within seconds, they are all zigzagging backward like Cuddle-Lump.

"At your service! At your service!"

The other Hounds don't speak, but their barking changes to a remarkably Auntie Nithya–like cadence.

Then one of them knocks into Cuddle-Lump, tilting its head.

Buuurrrrppppp! "Even royalty burps!"

The rest of the Hounds do their best approximation of long, rolling burps.

"What's happened to my Hounds?" shouts the King.

"I believe they're just following the original sled-animal, Cuddle-Lump," says the Princess. "Perhaps if you turn them off, they could reset? Conserve energy for their return trip? Or perhaps they'll still follow their new leader?"

"Karina, you are not to mess with my Hounds! They serve the Kingdom!"

"So, apparently, does Cuddle-Lump."

54

Ela

BOTH LANDS

Ela's heart is threatening to pop right out of her chest. She's trying to sprint toward the Ice Marker, but everything – her legs, her stomach, her head, even the butterfly in her hand – is wobbly. Somewhere behind her the King is yelling. Ela forces herself forward.

There's a thump, and Ela looks back to see the Princess landing on her side of the fence. Spots start floating in front of Ela's eyes. *Not now, not now, not now.* Vertigsnow, again. Her body is pulling her down, and the butterfly is pulling away, and she's going to faint before she can use it to get home. She won't be able to pass through like she did this morning.

Except ... the realization pushes through the muddle and haze ... except she didn't have the butterfly this morning. She lost it last night, and she passed through the Mist anyway. *Something from this land, something from that.* Or something from both.

The butterflies, yes ... but also Ela. She's from both lands too.

Like the butterflies, she flutters and shakes whenever she's at a passing point between the two lands. That's what happened by the Mists and by the water mixing in the Meander River. It happened her first time by the Ice Marker and it's happening again now. In her, though, the shaking is vertigsnow. To pass to the other land, all she needs is herself.

She sees that the Princess's arm is stretched out toward her to help steady her. They take the last steps together.

"Yours," manages Ela. She pushes the butterfly into the Princess's hand.

The Princess shakes her head. "You need it to get home."

"Yours," Ela repeats. "If you want another future."

There's another thump. The King has made it over the fence too. He's running now, his royal robe flapping behind him. Ela inhales the cool evening air.

"You have the butterfly. You have the Book. You have a choice," Ela says to the Princess.

"Eelie..."

But Ela's out of time. She stumbles forward and lets herself fall.

55

Ela

STILL SIX

The Snow covers her loosely, like a quilt, then squeezes her tight like a hug, then releases her to the tunnel. Ela's falling, and she can't see a thing, but it's not vertigsnow, it's a roller-coaster thrill, her stomach in her chest, her mouth in an O, and the press of air all around. She waits for the bottom, but it doesn't come, and the dropping starts to feel more like drifting.

Ela takes a deep breath. The air is moist. She's in a cave, after all, carved from the water in both lands, but the smell has turned from Snow to snow. Her head is clearer now, and memories float in and out: her father explaining that caves like this exist, the Princess carrying her up a huge hill, her mom's voice in this in-between space, calling after her.

Now there's light, a speck at first, but growing larger and larger. Her free fall morphs into a glide. The tunnel flattens, like the bottom of a slide, and she slows to a stop.

Ela steps out just where she hoped she'd land, at the

mouth of one of the caves by her house. It's snowing, and already the ground is covered, though only with an inch or two. The streetlights from her neighbourhood shine in the distance. She can't wait to get home and call her parents. But first, she catches a falling snowflake and counts.

One, two, three, four, five, six. Six sides, six points. All still.

She thinks of the Princess. Then she blows at the snowflake and makes a wish.

56

The Princess

FOOTPRINTS

The Princess stares at the spot in the Snow where Ela disappeared. It's filling in slowly, carefully, as if it's waiting for something more. But Ela's not coming back. The Princess knows that as sure as she knows anything.

"The girl is gone," says the King behind her. "Thanks to your foolishness."

A very small part of her deflates at the disapproval in his voice. Muscle memory, perhaps. But the bigger, better part of her wants to tell him it wasn't foolishness at all. No matter what happens, she's proud of this choice. She turns to face him, but before she can speak, his eyes widen and his mouth twists in a smile.

"Well, well, well. Perhaps you can make amends after all."

The Princess realizes he's staring not at her, but at the corner of the Book that's peeking out of her coat.

"Based on what the girl said, it sounds like they still care for you. Perhaps enough to come back for you even without her here. It's time to trade your shovel for a pen. You've always been good with words," says the King.

The Princess isn't sure whether to laugh or cry. She understands. He wants her to write notes to convince Auntie Nithya and Uncle Neel that she needs rescuing. Maybe even notes to convince their subjects Mistmir is fit for habitation. She'll write and write, and he'll tinker with his Hounds and clutch the illusion of being King.

For a second, she considers flinging the Book as far as she can toward the Mists. There's a good chance she could throw it far enough that it would be buried before the King could reach it. On second thought, he'd probably have her dig for it.

"Just think, Karina. You could still be Queen one day. Imagine how you would be revered."

She doesn't need to imagine. She lived it for thirteen years. All the reverence in Mistmir couldn't make her any less lonely. She's tired of living in her past. If today has made her realize anything, it's that she wants a future. And maybe, even with her mistakes, she deserves one.

Time doesn't stand still. And neither will she.

She edges back to the space where Ela disappeared. The butterfly in her pocket buzzes eagerly as she kneels. Beside her, the King chuckles at her sentimentality. She lets him laugh.

The Princess drops the Book. The Snow does its best to swallow it, and she helps it along.

"That story ended a long time ago."

It's only when she rises empty-handed that the King seems to fully understand. Shock and fury cover his face. A wave of sadness washes over the Princess. Not because she regrets what she's done. But because this might be the last memory of her father, alone and angry, surrounded by the remnants of his deserted Kingdom.

She spins around and takes one long last look at the perfect Snow. It's so beautiful her throat catches. Maybe the Snow can change. Maybe her father too. She wonders if that was the real point of the Book – not the pages that were written, but the pages that are still blank.

"This way is still open if you ever decide there are things more important than being royalty," says the Princess. "You can find items from the Beyond Lands in the River Room and even on your Hounds."

The King grunts. The Princess takes the butterfly from her pocket. It's beating so fast in her hand she can hardly hold it. She steps forward and jumps.

Midair, she hears her father yell, "Noooooo!"

She isn't sure if it's for her or the Kingdom or himself. All she knows is that he has what he needs to make another choice.

The Snow catches her like a feather mattress, and then

she's falling through. She's in pure darkness, but within seconds the lightness in her body replaces any terror. Her dress balloons in the rushing air and so does her heart and there's the strangest sound echoing off the tunnel walls. It fills her from head to toe with such joy, she can hardly breathe. For a moment, she wonders if this is Ela's land always, though, no, that's impossible. But she wouldn't mind if it were. She lets herself float in the space, the sound still following her. She's lost all track of time when the darkness eases, the tunnel levels out, and she lands with a most inelegant thud. The sound is still there but softer, and it's only as she climbs out into the night that she realizes she is hearing her own laughter.

For a second, Karina feels like she hasn't travelled at all – the moon is still full, and there's snow on the ground – but then she sees the tops of tiny purple flowers and the first buds on the branches, all unbothered by the cold.

And then she finds what she was hoping for most of all: Ela's footprints, pressed in the snow, guiding her to a future still unwritten.

ACKNOWLEDGEMENTS

Endless gratitude to everyone who helped me transform the wisps of an idea into this book. It would not exist without you:

Molly Ker Hawn, you are the Auntie Nithya, Madame Vidya and Amma of agents all in one – fiercely loyal, deeply knowledgeable, and truly caring. Thank you.

My editor, Susan Van Metre, makes me a better writer and made *Snow* a better book. Thank you for your many insights that shaped my drafty drafts into the story they were meant to be.

I am grateful to everyone at Walker Books and Candlewick Press who worked on this book and helped launch it into the world, including Lindsay Warren, Christine Engels, Pete Matthews, Stephanie Pando, Katie Ring, Betsy Uhrig, Maggie Deslaurier, Emily Quill, Sarah Chaffee Paris, Poppy David, and Madison Karpiej. Special thanks to jacket artist Cornelia Li, Maya Tatsukawa, in-house designer Lissi Erwin, and art director Maria Middleton for the breathtaking cover and delightful interior of the US edition. Many thanks to the Walker UK team for the stunning UK edition, especially Emily McDonnell, designer Maia Fjord, and cover illustrator Alexis Snell.

Alison Green Myers helped me with this book though its entire journey – from brainstorming to page proofs – and Mare Hagarty, Sarah Kapit and Maria Frazer gave me valuable feedback at crucial points along the way. Thank you all for your insights, your encouragement, and most of all, your friendship.

I'm grateful to my writing communities, including the Writer's Center, where I first started taking classes and developing my craft, and the Highlights Foundation, which is a continual source of learning, inspiration and connection.

I am beyond lucky to be surrounded by loving, funny, and endlessly supportive friends and family who make my life and my work better. Thank you all for being a part of my life, and, as always, special thanks to my parents, Adarsh and Ranvir Trehan.

Maya and Curran, you are such fun, interesting, loving people, and you make my world brighter and bigger. There's no way I'd be able to come up with the stories I do without you.

Curt, thank you for everything, and especially the many conversations about the scientific properties of magical snow.

ABOUT THE AUTHOR

MEERA TREHAN is the author of *The View from the Very Best House in Town*. She grew up in Virginia, just outside Washington, DC. After attending the University of Virginia and Stanford Law School, she practised law for over a decade before turning to creative writing. She lives in Maryland with her family.